SUNSET RIM

Center Point
Large Print

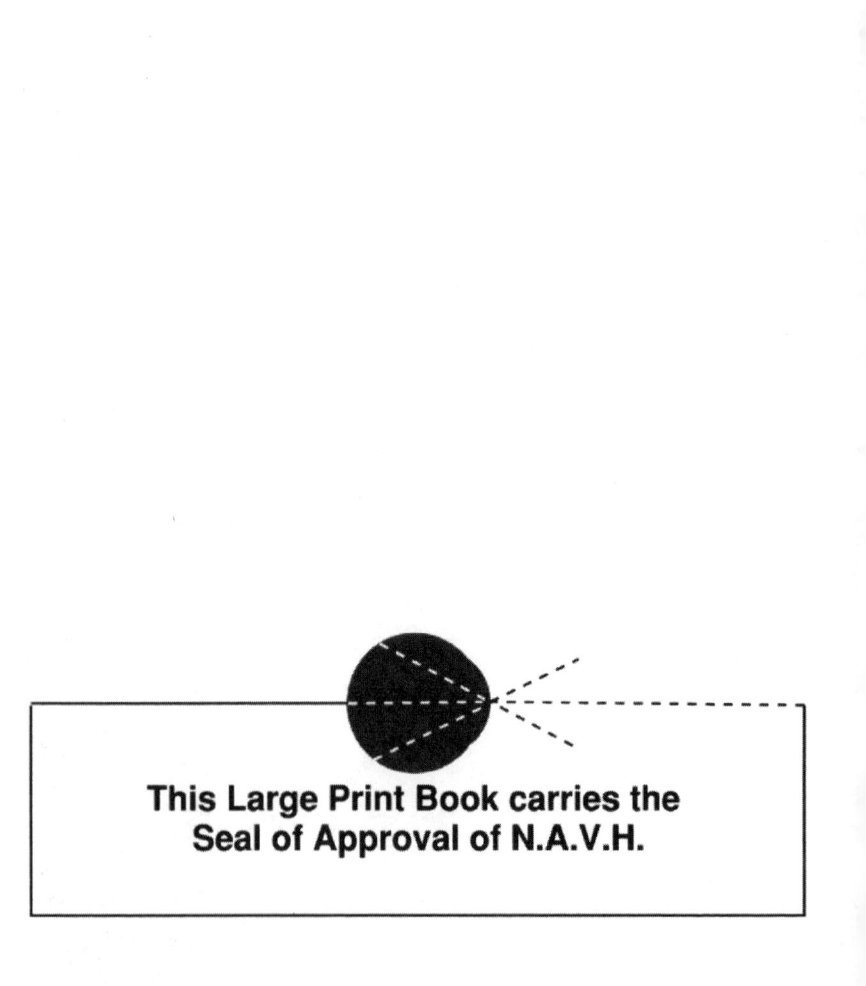
This Large Print Book carries the
Seal of Approval of N.A.V.H.

SUNSET RIM

Curtis Bishop

CENTER POINT PUBLISHING
THORNDIKE, MAINE

This Center Point Large Print edition
is published in the year 2010 by arrangement with
Golden West Literary Agency.

The text of this Large Print edition is unabridged.
In other aspects, this book may vary
from the original edition.
Printed in the United States of America
on permanent paper.
Set in 16-point Times New Roman type.

ISBN: 978-1-60285-857-2

Library of Congress Cataloging-in-Publication Data

Bishop, Curtis Kent, 1912–
Sunset rim / Curtis Bishop. — Center Point large print ed.
p. cm.
ISBN 978-1-60285-857-2 (large print : lib. bdg. : alk. paper)
1. Large type books. I. Title.
PS3503.I7835S86 2010
813′.54—dc22

2010016170

TO GRAHAM

for many reasons

1

AT THE MOMENT there was nothing about this sprawling town to bring back a flood of memories. It was like a hundred other towns he had ridden into at dusk on a hundred other nights. The expected thrill of coming back home simply wasn't there.

Were all towns etched in this same colorless unimaginative pattern—a street was a silver streak between low buildings whose square fronts and overhanging board awnings had long ago lost the gloss of fresh paint; a blacksmith shop, the smell of its forge fire hanging in the still air; lights shining out of dusty windows and locust trees forming an irregular line along the walks? Saddle horses stood here and there before hitch-racks and the wide mouth of a stable yawned at him, with a lantern swinging in its arch. Here he turned and dismounted, seeing two men tipped against the stable wall in their chairs. The lantern light showed the pale attention of their eyes.

Neither of them spoke. He said "putting up," and waited for some answer—a recognition, an invitation to talk. One could not but do more. Ed Kane shrugged his shoulders and strode along the board walk until he met the edge of another street running out of the shadows. On the four corners of the square thus created stood a saloon, a hotel, a feed store and an empty building. Even if he had never been in Cotulla before, he would have known where to find the hotel. It stood across the dust from him and he could hear the clatter of dishes and the buzz and talk in the dining room.

He crossed the street and entered the hotel's narrow lobby. One man sat in the semi-darkness, the glow of his cigarette half revealing his face. He gave the newcomer a surly nod and came slowly and stiffly to his feet, seemingly half-resentful of this intrusion upon his solitude.

"Only one room left," he said curtly. "Number eight. Supper will be over in thirty minutes. Better hurry."

"Thanks."

The newcomer took the dirty dull-pointed pen and wrote "Ed Kane." The hotel clerk reversed the register, pulling wire-rimmed spectacles out of his pocket and cocking them precariously on his nose. He studied the name and his lips moved faintly. He betrayed no excitement or surprise—hotel clerks in a range country town are never surprised or excited. But it was obvious that he knew the name, and was impressed by it.

"I'll wash up," said Kane, "then be right down to supper."

The stairway swayed a little when he put his weight on it. On the dark upper landing he turned uncertainly in a narrow hall and struck a match before finding an unlocked door. A key would be provided if he insisted. Otherwise his door would remain unlocked. Inside were a wash basin and a stained towel. Kane dabbed at his face, brushed back his coal-black hair, straightened his kerchief and carefully dusted his Stetson. Then, ready for supper, he descended the stairs again.

He cut into the dining room and took one of the vacant tables. On a blackboard hanging on the opposite wall somebody had written: "Menu—T-Bone and Mashed Potatoes—Apple Pie. Fifty cents."

There were other men in the dining room. At a huge rear table twelve of them sat together, with a man who was obviously a deputy sheriff sitting apart from them, munching placidly on a scoop of pie he held in his gnarled hands. Ed Kane recognized them as a jury. He searched their faces—surely he must know some of them. He had been gone from Cotulla only six years—he couldn't have completely forgotten the people of his county in such a short time. When he left he had known everyone in the Frio Valley, even to the lower flats beyond the Conroy spread where few boys, and fewer men, ever went.

Some he could recognize, not from remembrance of them as individuals but because he could recall family characteristics—the high cheekbones of the foreman who must be a Winslow, either Ellis or Keith; the tight lips of a broad-shouldered man who must be a Cumberland, one of Matthew's six sons. Some returned his curious glance but not an eye lighted in recognition. Perhaps Ed Kane had changed in six years. Certainly he was leaner. And six years as a Texas Ranger smooths out the laughter wrinkles of youth and etches in new and deeper lines, which make a face seem different even though its overall pattern has been unchanged.

Then another deputy came into the restaurant and sat down across the dining hall. With him was a man obviously his prisoner, who was half boy and half man, with the eyes and cheeks of one and the sharp mouth of the other. It took Ed Kane a long minute to recognize the prisoner.

When he did, it was with a start and a grin. Tom McGee had been only a button when he rode away, a grinning button who rode the wildest steers at rodeos and whose devil-may-care stunts enlivened every Fourth of July celebration. He was one of the many McGees who eked out a precarious living on the high ridges of the rim, half farmers, half cattle raisers. And, Kane could add from his own knowledge, half thieves. Cotulla had always said of Tommy McGee that he was the best of a bad lot.

Now the girl was standing by his table to take his order. Ed looked up with an apologetic smile.

It died on his lips. He could remember this girl. Hers was the type of dark hair one doesn't forget, curly as a mare's mane, soft and glistening. The eyes beneath were blue pools, placid and bottomless. He could remember the hair and those eyes. He had lifted her onto a corral fence and teased her about them and she had looked at him gravely and shyly, but unafraid.

"Mary!" he exclaimed gently. "Don't you remember me?"

She was staring at the table where the deputy sat with the handcuffed man. She turned at his speech and a smile came to her lips.

"Why, Ed Kane!"

He studied her intently. Something had happened to Mary McGee in these six years. He could guess at it, and he didn't like what he guessed. What had happened leaped up as a barrier between them, chilling the warmth of his greeting and of her recognition, for each of them was quickly afraid that the other would misinterpret a warmth that was purely friendship.

Ed looked away—a man's shyness shows so much more plainly than a woman's—and his gaze fell upon the handcuffed man. "Tommy?" he asked gravely.

"Yes."

"What's the charge?"

"Rustling."

"No!"

"Why not?" shrugged Mary. There was a quirk to her lips that deadened the beauty he remembered in her girlhood, which had held over into even a bitter maturity. "You know the McGees have always killed cattle when they wanted meat. We've done it for years."

Kane nodded. That was true. But the McGees had never been thought of as rustlers. They were no-good people, no worse. They lived in run-down shacks wherever men let them and they came down in the valley only when there were dances and celebrations and the talents of the McGees as fiddlers and mimics were in demand. Every McGee could play a fiddle and a banjo and sing.

"Who brought the charge?" he asked. Almost every range had families living on its borders who killed beef that didn't belong to them. Usually there was no protest as long as they never killed more than they could eat.

"The Conroys, of course."

"Tommy musta been off his home fence line to kill the Conroy beef," Kane murmured, a question in his eyes if not in his tone.

"They've pushed up the valley," shrugged Mary McGee. "'Way up the valley. Do you want the dinner?"

"Yes."

"Cream in your coffee?"

"No, black."

Mary turned toward the kitchen. His gaze followed her and he sighed. Mary McGee had been his favorite of the younger girls in the valley who had hung on his footsteps whenever he came to town, worshiping him as the valley's best rider and cowboy, and then as the valley boy who went away to become a Texas Ranger.

It was not strange that he so quickly saw what had happened. And she confessed it, with neither of them speaking a word in this relation. There was no such thing as a false front in this country. It had ugly qualities, too many ugly qualities, but not subterfuge.

Other people pushed into the dining room. Evidently Tommy McGee's trial held the interest of the countryside. Some of these men Ed Kane remembered, but there was no answering recognition. The table where the young thin-lipped prisoner sat with the deputy caught their interest like a magnet. Ed Kane recalled other towns where an insignificant occurrence smoldered up into violence. Something here was tight. Something here was thin and odd. A feeling brushed across Kane's senses and sent his gaze roving from one table to another, and then back to the open doorway where now four people stood, their entrance as dramatic as if staged.

He knew these people too. He knew all of them—and yet he didn't. There was Calhoun Conroy, who had not changed—Calhoun, who stood with a pride running up and down his back like a steel rod, Calhoun, who glared around him imperiously, as if angry that there was not an empty table when he wished to use one, as if piqued that other people dared to sit when he,

Calhoun Conroy, had to stand. His eyes were black, and seemed blacker because of the majestic whiteness of his hair. His lips made an old man's bloodless line above his white goatee and the muscles of his jaws showed a stubborn bunching.

Kane could recognize Calhoun, and Jefferson Conroy who stood beside him—almost a replica of him, as tall and as grim; not as haughty, perhaps, but the lines in his young face indicated that that would come.

But behind the Conroys, whom he had never liked but yet had never hated in the bitter unreasonable way the valley hated them, stood a broad-shouldered, dark-eyed man who wore black broadcloth and waved a cigar. Ed's lips softly murmured, "Carter Slade." In this last hour he had seen many persons he remembered. Among them was Mary McGee, at least, whom he wanted to see again. But Carter Slade was the first face that brought memories rushing back, that made this seem again like the Cotulla of his boyhood instead of another western town etched from an ugly, unimaginative key pattern.

Carter Slade's was the first face he had seen which made him stand up with a confident smile on his lips. The others might remember and might not—he did not care to take a chance. With Carter there was no doubt.

Now Carter saw him, and the heavy eyebrows lifted immediately. Carter took a step forward with the gleam in his eyes that Ed had been sure of seeing. As suddenly it faded. Carter kept coming, but now there was an impassiveness about his strong features that disturbed Kane.

"Glad to see you, Kane," Carter said, shaking his hand firmly but with no warmth. "Heard you were coming back."

Ed concealed his disappointment well. He should have known better than to expect Carter Slade to be elated over his return. They had covered this valley as youngsters, sleeping together in oak-shaded valleys and hunting high on rocky crags. But that had been a long time ago and Carter Slade had turned on to other things.

Evidently he had done well. Pressing behind him were the Conroys, and there was Catherine Conroy standing right before Kane, six years older than when he had last seen her. She was more beautiful than ever but without the elusive appeal that had characterized her as a girl of eighteen, when Ed Kane danced with her at the few functions a daughter of Calhoun Conroy could attend. He had told her lightly that she was the prettiest girl in the valley.

She recognized him, he could tell that. But her dark eyes considered him without friendliness. She wore fawn-colored riding trousers and they helped to make her seem tall, although actually she came only to Kane's chin, and was no taller than Carter Slade, who was a short man. She wore a man's shirt open at the neck. It fell carelessly away from her throat and showed the smooth, ivory shading of the skin. Her lips were long and her eyes wide-spaced and of a gray that had no bottom. She gave him the impression of having matured emotionally as well as physically, since he had seen her last.

"Oh, hello, Ed," she said lightly. "It seems to be crowded here, doesn't it?"

"It is," he admitted. The cruelest cut that can be given to a man who has been gone a long time is to recognize him, and then to act as if he had never been away.

Now Calhoun Conroy and his son were pressing behind Carter and Catherine. Two men at the next table gulped their coffee hurriedly.

"Just a minute, Mister Conroy—you can have this table."

Calhoun tilted his head slightly and waited stoically for them to finish. Kane sank back into his chair. Mary set his dinner before him and he saw how her hands trembled. She spilled coffee into his saucer.

"Oh, I'm sorry," she apologized. "I'll bring you another cup."

"I usually drink out of my saucer anyhow," he smiled.

He shot a glance across the dining room at Tommy McGee. The prisoner was eating slowly. His gaze roving the room seemed to be dancing in merriment. But Kane was not deceived by this. His way of life had sent him on the trail of many such youths. This type of boy was already a pattern old to the West. Always laughing, bubbling gaiety personified. But that laughter was only on the surface and did not hide, from men who knew, the coldness and the bitterness beneath. Ed Kane's closest call had been with such a boy. He still carried the slug in his shoulder, he whose shooting was a Ranger legend.

Tommy had not laughed until the Conroys entered the room. Now everything he saw impressed him as being funny.

Kane bent his head over the steak. He had forgotten that the Frio Valley was like this. Distance had lent it enchantment. Too, his family had never figured in the feud that evidently still raged unchecked. High in the upper valley his father had tended to his own herds, minding his own business and crisply inviting his neighbors to do the same, speaking to them and visiting with them, but never sharing with them, or inviting them to share with him. Then, at his death, Kane had gone to the Rangers and Sully to Wyoming. Thus the Kanes had always been as completely neutral as anybody in this valley could be, even to the sons. Ed was like that now, resentful of the way Catherine Conroy had treated him, yet willing to forget what might have been an unintentional slight.

But it wasn't a slight. She was looking at him closely, studying his face bent over his plate.

Carter Slade also was studying him. So were the two Conroy men, Calhoun with his white eyebrows drawn in a sharp line. They evidently were talking about him—Carter was making a motion with his head.

Kane finished eating and called for another cup of coffee. He rolled a cigarette without looking up from his plate. Nor did he look up until a voice in his ear said, "Kane."

"Hello, Mister Gilbert," Kane said, standing up.

Gilbert shook his hand warmly, almost pumping it. He was an owlish-faced little man with bristling gray whiskers. He had a sort of mongrelishness about his face, which peeped out of his beard. His long hair was like a chestnut thrusting its head through its bur. But Jeremiah Gilbert was a strong man—if he was not strong in the way of this western country, with his horse and his rope and his gun, he was still strong with a shrewdness and a capacity for trade no other man in this valley possessed, or wanted. Even in Kane's youth Jeremiah Gilbert, because of his shrewdness, was master of the upper valley. Where the Conroys ruled the lower valley with haughty ruthlessness, Jeremiah reigned because of a capacity for business.

"I see you got my letter," said Jeremiah, sinking into a chair and accepting Ed's offer of coffee.

"Yes," Kane admitted.

That letter had surprised him. There was no reason for Jeremiah Gilbert to invite him back to the Frio Valley and offer a substantial loan to build a house and throw up corral fences and stock his range. Perhaps Jeremiah had liked his father, one could never tell. But certainly Henry Kane had never been fond of Jeremiah Gilbert.

"Well, do you want the range?" barked Jeremiah, bobbing his head impatiently. "It's good land there."

"I've been trying to make up my mind," smiled Ed. "I'm sentimental about the place, yes. I was raised there, and my dad loved it until his dying day and nobody could ever convince him that, for year-in and year-out grazing, he didn't have the best pasture in the valley. But I'm a little uneasy about your offer, Mister Gilbert. If I remember aright, you were plumb anxious for Sully and me to sell out."

"I'm running my stuff further back on the rim," shrugged Gilbert. "I want you back because nesters are creeping in. I'd rather have a friend crowding me back from the river than an enemy."

"Well, I'll think about it," Ed grinned.

"Don't wanna rush you into anything," Jeremiah grumbled. But the disappointment in his voice showed very plainly that Jeremiah did want a quick decision.

Kane laid his half dollar on the table as he started out. He wanted to leave a tip for Mary McGee, but he decided against it. There was a tilt to her chin which screamed out that she wanted neither Ed

Kane's patronage nor his sympathy. It was just as well—he could give neither.

He walked into the saloon next door where other faces were familiar. Soon he was in pleasant conversation with Ellis Winslow, Maury Cumberland and the Upshaw boys from over the rim. They chatted with him cordially, but he sensed the strange reserve in their manner and the deliberate abstinence from asking about his plans that was typical of this country, and always would be. Behind the bar stood a wizened little man, obviously of Tommy McGee's blood. But it took Kane a long time to place him—the eldest McGee boy, Jerry, who had also been away.

Jerry wiped the bar in front of Kane as the Winslows and Upshaws drifted out.

"So you're back, Mister Kane!" he said softly. "I'm glad. You're just the man for this valley."

There had always been a hint of humbleness about Jerry McGee—none of the defiant laughter that was Tommy's, or the pride that had been Mary's, that she could still show to some people—like Ed Kane.

"What do you mean, Jerry?"

"I ain't talkin'," shrugged the bartender, glancing furtively over one shoulder. "Talk never pays off anybody, least of all here."

He slid down the bar to pour a whisky for a tall, sharp-eyed man who had just come in. Ed gave this man a curious glance. He was not a native of the valley or, if so, he had moved in recently. A man who has been a Ranger knows how to size up another man. Ed Kane liked him, and yet didn't.

Ed received a pleasant nod. "You must be Kane. Have one on me?"

"Sure," Ed said instantly, sliding down the bar and nodding to Jerry.

This man had clear gray eyes—eyes used to looking into long distances—and a faint smile on his lips as if he were slightly amused about something.

"Heard of you with the Rangers," he said. "As far west as Arizona. You made a name for yourself, Kane."

"Yeah," drawled Ed, holding up his glass and gesturing with it.

The man seemed to be making fun of him. This man was not afraid of him for what he had been with the Texas Rangers. He wore two six-guns very low and the right hand was stained darker than the left, which meant he wore no glove on the hand he liked to use. Yet the shifty look which marked a rustler or a cheap killer was absent. This man probably was wanted somewhere for a crime that he had likely committed. But at that, he was not afraid of, and did not regret, the trail he rode.

"Understand you're coming back here. Going to re-stock your dad's old range and settle down?"

"It's about time," Ed nodded. "Life doesn't hold

out much to a man who has been on the trail. You should know that—?"

There was question in the lift of his voice. The gray-eyed man smiled.

"Purdy, Peck Purdy."

Kane liked him for his frankness. Peck Purdy was a wanted man in Arizona—the Rangers had been asked three years ago to be on the lookout for him. Yet Peck blandly gave his right name. He knew the Rangers were like that, especially a man who is just a former Ranger. Let Arizona worry about what Peck Purdy did there.

Texas was a different place, and Purdy a different man—until he tipped his hand. Now Purdy was studying his empty whisky glass. "Sorry to hear that, Kane," he drawled. "I don't see anything ahead but trouble if you try to move onto your dad's old spread."

"Who from?"

"The boss. Or should I say the bosses?"

"Who are they?"

"Don't you know?" Purdy asked innocently. "I ride for Carter Slade. And all of us, of course, work for the Conroys."

Ed was silent a moment. He had seen this association between Carter Slade, his old friend, and the Conroys, and it had strongly impressed him.

"Carter and I got along swell years ago," he said slowly. "I think we still can."

"Mebbe," Purdy nodded.

Kane raised his glance. Those gray eyes were gazing straight at him and Peck Purdy seemed to be mocking him. "I think mebbe," he said, "I can get along with you, Purdy. This one's on me."

Purdy accepted. "Here's to that—" he proposed, "that we get along."

2

A VERDICT was expected before noon. Kane didn't go to the courthouse for the morning session, in which both counsels made their pleas to the jury. Instead, he rode along the gurgling Frio, at times narrow enough for his horse to jump across in this dry season, climbing higher and higher against the massive rim which sat looking down upon the valley with indifferent majesty.

Coming out of the timber about ten o'clock, he was at the rim of a narrow valley lying north and south, almost perpendicular with the whimsical Frio and parallel with the base of the bleak-faced rim which was actually not a single rim at all, but a succession of rocky tiers one after another. A road skirted up the river. River and road both disappeared around a bend farther south, where hills seemed to squeeze the valley thin.

He reached the road and followed it around that bend. Cattle grazed in the narrow meadows. He studied their brands and recognized this valley as an overrun of three or four spreads—Gilbert's cattle and also the Winslows'.

The road went definitely upward until, at the end of a half hour's climb, he skirted one more twin and saw the colorless crumbling house he had left behind six years before. The corrals were tottering—a single steer could push them over. But the spring was still there and he was grateful for the cold sweetness of its water, as he had always been.

This was a small valley. Henry Kane had always said it was too small for a big cattle family and had encouraged his sons to seek out spreads of their own. The hills on either side, and the rim behind, set it apart from the neighboring ranges. Yet, Ed could recall, both Jeremiah Gilbert and Calhoun Conroy had wanted it. It was good winter range for a small herd. Freezes and drouths never completely wiped out a man here. He could sell down to what the valley could forage and the next spring start over again.

Certain things a man forgets to remember for a time, but sooner or later they flood back upon him. Here Kane's mother had died. Her grave must be by the willows back of the spring, though the ground had been washed level by many a spring rain breaking down the rimside in straggling fugitive torrents. Until he had looked at this spot he could not be sure that he wanted to give up his

Ranger star forever, and forget, here in this sameness of a single valley, other valleys that other trails led into, and—for some—led out of.

Jeremiah Gilbert's letter had interested Ed Kane immediately. It had impressed upon him what all the Rangers talked about in their few leisure hours, that theirs was a life for a young man; that for an older man even a life as hard as theirs could not go on forever; and that the more a man became known for his six-gun speed and accuracy the more he was challenged to prove it, until sooner or later it was bound to fail him.

That, more than the loneliness and the hardship, had tempted Ed Kane to give up his star. At first his reputation had not been an empty thing, but as one man's triumph over the forces around him which made this skill and speed essential to existence. He had gloried in it as a man glories in the camp he has flung up against the cold and rain of the night and the sparkle of his self-made campfire that preserves and insures his comfort, while the beasts of the wild can do nothing but suffer and endure. For a while he had lived in this smugness, never boasting and never rushing into a fight, but never avoiding one, and never thinking beforehand that this one could well be his last, that every string sooner or later runs out. Then he became impressed with its futility, and was embittered. He raged against the feeling of helplessness within him, the sense of resignation that kept him going even though he hated it, that made honest men and crooks look alike to his tired eyes.

There was a boy much like Tommy McGee—that same sort of nervous laugh, the same sort of beardless innocence. The crime was trivial, as was Tommy's. But the boy laughed at the deputy sheriff sent to arrest him and, after that, the crime was serious—among lawmen there necessarily must be an unspoken vow to settle the death of their own. An owl-hoot rider cannot be conceded the privilege of shooting down in fair fight a man sent to bring him back. When one lawman dies another must take the trail, and still another—until finally, inevitably, goes out the man who can bring the outlaw in. It added to Ed Kane's unhappiness that he came to be among the last sent out. For this boy who had been like Tommy McGee, he *was* the last.

That hurt itself could have healed over, if the memory hadn't hung on. It was the way the boy came out to meet him, joyously unafraid, challenging Ed Kane as the personification of an alien force he did not understand, but was not unwilling to face. The boy grandiloquently sent boasting word he would meet this famous Ranger face to face, and would settle whatever lay between them man to man.

Other Rangers became hardened to that. Ed never was. There was nothing between this boy and Ed Kane. Ed could have liked him, as he still liked Tommy McGee, even if Tommy had killed a beef which belonged to a man who resented his steers being killed for beef by people such as the McGees. But, when such a challenge was hurled in his face, Kane could not step aside nor could he shoot wild in the face of a shot that came hurtling at his heart.

Then he received Jeremiah's letter. Ed turned in his star with the promise that, if he didn't stay in Cotulla and the Frio Valley, he would return. Until Gilbert's letter, it had never occurred to him to return. He was merely tempted at first. But the sight of this benchland, with the green moss overgrowing the rocks around the spring, stirred him. Its charm gripped him. Yet the loneliness was heavy around him and he couldn't help but wonder if a man like him, restless and virile, could live there alone, with no company except the faces that came leaping up at him out of a past no less bitter because it had been just.

Smoking as he sat like an Indian on his haunches, Ed Kane thought it out. Just as he made up his mind, he heard footsteps. There was no reason why he should step back among the willow branches, but he did. Perhaps it was habit, an instinct which men riding his kind of trails necessarily acquire.

Anyhow, the rider coming toward the cabin did not see him. From a long way off Ed realized it was a woman, and his eyebrows knitted into question marks. Soon he recognized her. No one else had that curly black hair.

He let her go into the cabin, then followed her inside. He surprised her as she stood studying a note which she had hung on a rusty nail behind the doorway.

Prying subconsciously, he read the note over her shoulder before she could turn around.

"I can't meet you anymore," it read.

She gasped as she realized his presence. His noiseless walk was also habit.

Fright left her eyes and defiance entered when she recognized him.

"Well, Ed Kane, are you satisfied?"

"I'm sorry, Mary," he said gently. "I didn't intend to read it."

"It's not your affair," she said stiffly. "Nor shall I tell you whom it's for."

"I don't even want to know," he denied.

The storm left her face and she seemed ill at ease. Obviously Mary McGee was not accustomed to apologies. She toyed with her riding gloves.

"I have only a minute," she murmured. "The verdict is due about noon."

Ed nodded. "Intending to ride back myself."

He helped her into the saddle and she thanked him with a flicker of her blue eyes.

"You always were the gallant one, Ed," she said. "Being in the Rangers didn't change you."

Kane shrugged his sloping shoulders. His former buddies would get a kick out of that!

The sun was high over the rimtop and they would have to ride hard to reach the courthouse by noon. The smell of pine and stunted cedar was sweet in Ed's nostrils and he gloried in the view below him, as they rode along the high path. He hated to turn down the bluff, to weave closer and closer to the settlement that lay on the riverside like an ugly infestation. Kane hated towns. Association with other men, and women, seemed to bring out the worst in a man, never the best. More men were killed on the dusty streets of such towns than on all the ranges put together. And the fights in the open were usually the anti-climax of a sore that had festered inside a town.

The courthouse was shaded by cottonwood trees with bits of sun-starved grass beneath. Around the square were drawn up the rigs of nearly every ranch in the valley. Ed could name them off—the Rolling X, the Straight T, the Slanting Y, and the Crown, of course. Saddle horses were hobbled to the rickety three-wire fence protecting the courthouse lawn from foraging cattle, as if any self-respecting cow would not turn its back upon dusty Cotulla and head for the sweet fresh range beyond!

Here were more people than Kane had ever seen in Cotulla, except for the holiday rodeos or a political speaking. They sat on the steps, whittling or chewing, rolling smokes with slow deliberate motions, looking away most of the time, talking only in sparse syllables. He and Mary tethered their horses to the elm stump in front of the main gate and walked slowly up the steps. Men looked up and knew them, but not all spoke. Those greetings they did receive were quick and suspicious.

Again Ed sensed the tenseness, the enmity, the smoldering fire. A man who did know this setting from the past could have walked through them without consciousness of their feelings, for the gravity of their hatred lay lightly on their dark, high cheekbones and was expressed only in their intent looks and their straight lips.

Tommy McGee's trial had taken on an exaggerated importance. Inside, glancing at the faces of the jury, Kane understood the tenseness, and why Carter Slade and a dozen Crown riders were there, why Catherine Conroy sat proud and straight on the front row. A day ago Tommy McGee had been a friendless waif, a no-good boy out of a no-good tribe, acceptable at times for his fiddling and his yodeling but usually outcast for his laziness and impudence. Had an upper-valley man brought the charge, Tommy McGee's conviction would be certain, though the jurymen might have shrugged their shoulders and admitted it was a little harsh to send a young'un up just for killing for a side of beef.

But no upper-valley man had brought the charge. It was the Crown Ranch and Calhoun Conroy. The jury of upper-valley men had accepted the challenge, and all of Frio Valley was there to see it thrown back into the face of Calhoun Conroy and his family, which included Slade and Purdy and the other lean, harsh men who never stayed long, regardless of what Calhoun was willing to pay.

Looking at the jury, and feeling the ripple around him, Ed Kane knew that Tommy McGee would go free.

The prisoner sat loose-jointed, half lounging in his chair, apparently pleased at being the center of attention, evidently not caring a continental damn what the jury said or didn't say. Ed looked at him and wanted to recommend clemency. To give that grinning, devil-may-care boy a brief stretch in the pen for this insignificant crime would be to turn loose a hellion when the penitentiary gates swung open and he was free. It would take a stern Ranger to track him down then—perhaps several of them. It was this type of criminal which troubled Kane most, this type which had driven him out of the Rangers.

Kane sat down with Mary. He knew what the looks shot in his direction meant, what the women were thinking when they glared and then looked away.

"Brazen hussy! She doesn't take much time! Just as soon as Ed Kane lands in town she makes a play for him! Well, better a rounder like Kane than a married man! Mebbe she will stay so busy with him she won't have time to go around breaking up homes."

For some reason, a madcap spirit swept over Ed Kane, as unreasonable in its defiance as that which caused Tommy McGee to rise at the judge's instruction and face his jury with a broadening grin. Kane even bent over and whispered to Mary. He had nothing to say. It was to make the gesture here where all could see.

But many eyes had missed the by-play. The foreman of the jury was clearing his throat—Matthew Cumberland, a cousin of the Cumberlands who lived almost at the upper end of Sunset Rim.

"We, the jury, find the defendant—not guilty!"

There was no ripple of applause. There were grins, yes. The sentiment of the courtroom was in hearty endorsement of this verdict. Tommy McGee turned to his deputy and slapped him on the shoulder and grinned again, as if to say: "So long, *amigo*. It's been nice knowing you." Then he turned and started out of the courtroom before the others had risen from their seats. Kane pitied him, and yet approved the squareness of his shoulders and the tilt of his head. How like his sister he looked!

Then Kane looked across the courtroom and his eyes narrowed. The Crown men were leaving, staying close together. Carter Slade was in their middle, puffing on a cigar, his eyebrows in straight hard lines, his voice giving instructions to his men.

Peck Purdy went over to join his employer, walking with a swagger. It was like Peck Purdy not to stand with Carter Slade and the other Crown men, to snub his own kind thoroughly and coldly, to make it plain before everyone that the Crown received a kind of loyalty from him, yet only one kind.

A half dozen men gathered around Carter Slade. Ed did not know them as individuals, though he recognized their type at a glance. Hard-faced men. Ruthless men. Yet, appraising them, Kane knew that the dangerous men were Carter himself, smart in his own way but not smart enough to know the limitations of his cunning, and Peck Purdy, a lone wolf with a wolf's creed.

Catherine Conroy joined Carter in the doorway and the Crown riders moved away, all but Purdy. A barrier stood between the Conroys and their hired men. Other ranch families accepted line riders as social equals, eating and drinking with them privately and in public. The Conroys always kept the distinction there for the world to see. The better type of puncher never had worked for the Conroys—and never would.

Catherine did not seem so lovely to Ed Kane at this moment. Harshness hardened her features, as if she were older than the other valley girls—yet she must be younger by several months than Mary McGee, who fell back from Ed Kane's side as he started out.

Every woman was moving away. Only Catherine Conroy stood among the men folk who filled the courthouse vestibule to overflowing. Again Ed Kane felt the hidden tension in these grave, impassive men. He made an automatic gesture—he reached for the left pocket of his shirt. No star there to clutch and straighten. He was glad of it. If hell broke loose here it was no worry of his.

Jeremiah Gilbert gave him a wolfish grin. He answered with a curt nod.

"Made up your mind, Kane?"

"Just about," Ed said. "I'll be around to talk to you this afternoon. Where will you be—at the bank?"

"Yep, all afternoon."

Jeremiah was not only the biggest landholder in the upper valley but he was Cotulla's banker and leading cattle buyer. He lived in a dingy frame house while in town, but only because he was stingy. Actually he could buy and sell the Conroys without feeling the strain.

Kane sauntered into the middle of the Crown group. Perhaps he was making a play also, showing everyone here that he was neutral in this pending war, in this revival of a feud that no one in the valley had ever forgotten.

"Morning, Carter," he said pleasantly.

He looked to Purdy and nodded. Purdy returned the greeting.

Kane grinned at his former crony. "I rode up the rim today, Carter. It was great to see the old country. It's my dish from now on."

"You mean you're settling down there?" asked Carter.

"Figger on it," Ed nodded. "Going back to the old valley, Carter. Still has the best water in this country and the best winter grass."

"I believe I would think that over before making a final decision, Kane," Carter said brusquely. And "Kane," not "Ed." "Figure out why Jeremiah Gilbert is so anxious to have you back on your dad's old spread. Jeremiah outbid the Crown for your dad's interests. He was plumb anxious to have that land then. Don't it strike you as funny that he is anxious to get you back?"

"It did," Kane admitted. "I'm not a fool, Carter. But no other place would satisfy me. I was born here. The hills hold something for me. This Sunset Rim does. I'm buying the spread back from Gilbert."

"Are you crazy? Don't you see that the upper-valley people are trying to throw you against the Crown? You're their buffer, the great gunman who will shoot off the Conroy riders, and me. Are you pulling their chestnuts out of the fire, Kane?"

"No," Kane said slowly. "I know nothing about the squabble between upper and lower valley people. My dad always stayed out of it, and I reckon I can. Everybody in this valley is a friend of mine until I'm shown different. Isn't that fair enough, Carter?"

"We'll see," Carter grumbled. "We'll see."

The stocky man was obviously not disposed to argue further with Ed Kane. Ed tipped his hat to Catherine, gave Purdy another nod, and took the hint.

He was the second man out of the courtroom. The first, Tommy McGee, was lounging across the street in front of the restaurant. As men poured out of the courthouse in the wake of the Crown, Tommy went into the cafe. They could see him through the window drinking coffee, then buying a sack of tobacco and rolling a smoke.

Ed's lips quirked as he studied the milling crowd. It was easy to read the temper of these Crown men. The honor of their outfit had been violated. The court had ruled Tommy McGee innocent, but courts were still new to this land, that was not yet ready to accept such verdicts as final. There was another kind of law, the kind they had been raised by. There were still plenty of men who believed the old kind of law was the only kind which would ever hold this country.

The Crown had lost—in court. Not lost in life. Ed decided that summarily acquitting Tommy McGee was a mistake. This verdict was a challenge hurled into the teeth of the Crown and Calhoun Conroy was not the kind to back off from a challenge. Calhoun was not there himself, but his men were—scowling Carter Slade, who had changed while Kane was gone, and calm-eyed Peck Purdy.

The upper-valley men were the ones avoiding the challenge. They had hurled it, but they were leaving grinning Tommy McGee to bear its full brunt alone. They were standing back, staying in the courthouse, coming slowly out onto the lawn, letting the Crown men walk across the dusty street toward the cafe. Now Tommy came out of the cafe, still smoking his cigarette. The grin was still on his lips but his fingers were shaking.

Kane didn't like it. The Winslows and the Cumberlands and the Merricks—these men who had sat on the jury—were the ones flouting Calhoun Conroy's right to rule. Not Tommy McGee.

But Carter Slade and Peck Purdy were walking on while the other Crown men hung back, spreading out. The handwriting was there for anyone to read. The Crown was not backing away from a showdown.

The long silence held. McGee's fingers took the cigarette out of his mouth, put it back again. He could do nothing but wait, Kane thought. He had killed Crown beef—and suddenly this was a major affront to the Crown instead of just a minor nuisance. One jury had turned him loose, but here came another—judge and jury and prosecuting attorney and executioner all in one.

There was a growing sharpness in Tommy's shoulder-points until at last, when he could no longer endure it, he dropped the cigarette and pulled up his head and showed the gray, bitter color of his face. His shoulders dropped and he seemed to let a great breath out of him. Still he did not look directly at the two men striding slowly across the dust. When he did, Purdy or Slade would speak to him and gunshots would follow.

Ed Kane wanted to bolt forward, but he held himself back. This was a private fight. He was no longer a Texas Ranger sworn to uphold peace and order. He was a private citizen, a man who was going to live among these people, and who wanted no part of their blazing hatred. Neither side belonged to him and he belonged to neither side.

But, even as he deliberated, his feet were moving. He had a sympathy in his nature that few men in this country had, or dared express if it was in them. He could remember that other grinning kid coming out to meet him, as now Tommy McGee was walking across the dust to meet Peck Purdy.

He acted while he was still deliberating right and wrong. He stepped quickly across the courtyard and to Tommy's side.

"Got a match, Tommy?" he asked quietly, pulling an unlighted cigar out of his shirt pocket.

Tommy McGee stared at him unbelievingly. In long years of living in this valley no man had ever stepped to the side of a McGee. Except for the nights when their fiddles and the banjos were needed at dances, no one wanted the company of a McGee, except for the men who had wanted Mary. That seared deeper into the souls of the McGees than anything else.

With trembling fingers Tommy fished a match from a pocket. The grin that almost split his lips was a different kind of grin. A look came in his face that reminded Kane of a maverick calf lost in a snowbank and surrendering to the first hand which clutched it.

Never had Tommy been so glad to see a man. Never had he been so lonely as in those long seconds standing before the cafe, the accusing eyes of the countryside trained upon him, the slow steps coming closer and closer.

Now Kane turned. His calm eyes looked into the faces of Peck Purdy and Carter Slade.

He didn't say a word. Nor, for a long moment, did they. Then Carter Slade growled.

"Stand back, Kane. This ain't your range."

"Reckon I got a right to stand with a man who works for me, Carter," Ed drawled.

This stopped the swarthy foreman of the Crown. "Works for you?"

"That's right. Tommy McGee is riding for me."

His voice, though not loud, rang with the sharp intonations of a bell. In the second before Carter Slade answered, Kane saw Catherine Conroy's angry face, and the stormy fury of her eyes. She had seemed beautiful a moment before. Now she seemed only amusing.

Peck Purdy shrugged his shoulders. It was easy to guess Peck's train of thought. This was a new and unexpected adversary, one he did not take lightly. But Peck waited with inquisitive eyes on his employer's face and there was no doubt that a word from the broad-shouldered Slade would put him in action. He was that type of man, even when the other man was an Ed Kane.

But Carter Slade gave him no word. Carter stared at his old friend with eyes that blazed venom.

"You've dug your grave in this valley, Kane," he rasped. "Get ready for it."

"I'm ready," Ed said gently.

Tommy McGee pushed forward. "Make your play alone, Slade," he challenged. "Leave Kane out of it. And Purdy out of it. Stand on your own feet."

He came no higher than to Ed's shoulders and the grin had never left his face. His voice had a high girlish note as he delivered his challenge.

Kane made no motion toward his gun. If that was the way it would be, he would not take sides. If Tommy wanted it man to man, Ed would stay out of it.

It would come now—those watching in the courtyard were moving away to give them room.

But Carter didn't move. He still couldn't adjust himself to this new pattern. Slade showed them stunned wonderment, and they waited for him to say the only thing he could say. Never had a man been so challenged on a Cotulla street, and lived. Nobody accepted that kind of talk.

Carter Slade was not afraid. It was easy to see that even as he made no move toward his gun, even as he looked from McGee to Kane and back again, the muscles of his chest swollen and his upper lip twitching. He was not afraid and they knew it, but he backed down from the challenge of this flaming-eyed youngster who stood slight and defiant before him.

"You'll get yours, McGee," he threatened as he turned off. "Don't worry—you'll get yours. And you too, Kane. From now on it's war between us."

Ed moved his head slightly as if nodding. A sigh swept over the crowd in the courtyard as Carter Slade stalked toward his horse, Peck Purdy following at his heels, the other Crown riders straggling behind.

"Come on, McGee," Ed said harshly. "We need a drink to wash this dust out of our throats."

3

JEREMIAH GILBERT'S office was a hodgepodge of confused papers and magazines, of thumb-marked books and wooden boxes that served him in lieu of filing cabinets. His office reflected his stinginess—the unpainted pine table which served as a desk, the unwashed globe of the oil lamp, the rickety, straight-backed chairs which another man, even a poorer man, would have abandoned to the kindling pile. The entire bank likewise was as dingy and as cheap in its structure—rough board frame, uneven floors, iron bars in front of the single cashier's cage, rusted pen points that scratched so a man hardly could write his name.

But Kane was not deceived by these outward appearances. No one in the valley was. Jeremiah was a rich man and growing richer with the years. There were a fawning servility about him, a wheedling tone to his voice, a pleading gleam to his eyes. But his word had been law in the upper valley for ten years. Now he wanted to challenge the grazing rights of the Crown and come down the valley as far as the mouth of Culpepper Creek, daring to thrust his Ragged Cross brand over the Elbow Ridge. Sunset Rim lay at his back impassive, unyielding even before Jeremiah Gilbert. Ahead of him was the Conroy grass, and there were those who claimed Sunset Rim would abandon a fight before Calhoun Conroy ever would.

Not that Jeremiah grazed this land himself, or that the longhorns in the brush wore his brands. The Cumberlands, the Winslows, the Merricks, the Hardaways owned spreads in between and sent their line riders out almost to the shadow of Gilbert's corral. But this little stooped man with the thin, bristling whiskers owned those men as completely as Calhoun Conroy owned Carter Slade or Phil Mallory. He had lent them money against their spreads until they could be his at any time he cared to foreclose, and all of them knew it.

He had no intention of foreclosing. They paid him interest, high interest. And Jeremiah, among other things, was a cattle trader and shipper. He sold these men's cattle along with his own, never neglecting, of course, his commission. It suited Jeremiah for the Cumberlands and the Winslows and the Sloans to own their own herds. That saved him the trouble of hiring more riders and shouldering more responsibility. He did not even mind that these men who were his financial minions lived in better houses than he did, and wore better clothes, and even left Cotulla for San Antonio to blow good money on what Jeremiah considered the wildest kind of foolishness.

He was not a man of violence. He deplored the hot-headedness and the violence in this country. Calhoun Conroy had threatened to horsewhip him on sight and Jeremiah trembled whenever the dark-eyed Southerner was in town. His was the inspiration to bring Ed Kane back to the valley, to set him up in business along the benchland where his father had lived. That bench was a no-man's land now. It was government land, as was most of the mid-valley, and the grass belonged to the spread that could get its cattle there and keep them there. Now there was Crown beef on the bench along with some of Jeremiah's own stock and the Winslows'. But Jeremiah could get along without this winter range. The Crown couldn't.

"Well, Kane?" grinned the little man.

"I'm staying," Ed said curtly. "Let's draw up a deed to the house and corrals."

"You can have them," waved Jeremiah with strange generosity. "Falling down anyhow. Not worth much."

"No, it isn't," Ed agreed with a pang. Suddenly he felt he had neglected his duty by abandoning his father's home to the unfeeling Gilbert. He should have stayed there, instead of riding away with the Rangers.

"But the benchland back of the valley," Ed recalled. "That was Dad's land. He bought it at a government sale in Uvalde."

Jeremiah winced. He had purchased this for three dollars an acre from the older Kane. It wasn't prime grazing land. It was good only in lush seasons. When the rains were heavy, Henry Kane bought culls from other ranchmen and put them in the hills to fatten. Two years out of five it was good pasture. A man who played it for that would profit. Jeremiah had profited.

"Isn't the valley enough for a while?" he asked. "We can talk about the benchland later."

Kane shook his head. The valley was small and would run no more than a hundred head, year in and year out. This was enough to carry a small spread through a lean season. But a man going into the valley, which was government land, shut off on all sides by privately owned grass, was doomed to failure.

"I need all the benchland," Kane said crisply, "and probably a section or two of your timber country, Jeremiah."

No one ever heard of Jeremiah selling anything. He kept everything he ever owned, even back issues of magazines and periodicals that cluttered his office. It was on the tip of his tongue to refuse to sell, as he would have declined to sell to anyone but Ed Kane at any price. But it was essential to Jeremiah's plans that a strong man be planted at the creek mouth. The Crown, pushing up the Frio, would run smack into Ed Kane. They could not go around him. They either had to stop growing or to fight it out with him.

"I'll let you have the benchland," Jeremiah agreed. "Four dollars an acre."

"Three," Ed smiled coldly. "That's what you paid my dad."

"Three and a half."

"Three."

"All right, three," grumbled Jeremiah.

"And two dollars an acre for two sections of the timberland behind it," proposed Ed.

"No."

"No deal then," shrugged the lean man.

Jeremiah winced. He sensed Kane's stubbornness. Actually the former Ranger was enjoying himself. Not often could anyone force Jeremiah Gilbert to his own way of thinking.

"All right," he said weakly. He reached into a desk drawer and began to pull out blanks. Ed watched him laconically. All the valley let Jeremiah draw up all the papers. He was the only man in the valley who fully understood them. But, penny-pinching as he was, and as hard-driving, he was square with his papers. His deeds and title transfers would stand up in any court.

"You'll want stockers," Jeremiah murmured. "The Winslows are willing to let you have fifty head. And I'll sell you fifty, though I can't afford it."

"Prime stuff," Kane insisted. "We'll round up the cattle in the valley and I'll take my pick."

That was a harder bargain than it sounded. The cattle grazing along the creek bottom were the best in the Cotulla country. They were the young steers and stockers thrown onto the tall grass for fattening.

"No," Jeremiah said firmly, laying down his pen.

"You can't say that," Ed grinned. "The Crown will deal with me. They'll set me up on the creek bank and sell me land to the south and start me off with two hundred head."

Jeremiah's mouth flew open. He had not thought of that. Neither, as a matter of fact, had Kane. But a man in this country sometimes had to bluff. He couldn't be all bluff, for there was the strong surging temptation everywhere to call what might seem a bluff, and most bluffs were called. Jeremiah Gilbert would have called this one had it not been for the other circumstances.

"All right, a hundred head," he yielded. He scratched away, head almost touching the paper as he favored his myopic eyes. Finally he pushed the papers across to Kane for his signature.

"Ten per cent interest, Kane. That's business."

Ed pushed them back. "I'm not borrowing money, Jeremiah," he explained. "What is it in cash?"

"You got the cash?" Jeremiah exclaimed.

"I think so. There was some reward money with the Rangers, Jeremiah. I saved it."

Jeremiah groaned. This was the hardest blow of all. If Kane did not owe his bank, then Kane could dispose of his cattle as he saw fit, to any buyer or commission company. He would be free of the bonds of debt which Jeremiah had woven tight around the other valley families.

Gilbert started to pull the papers back. Ed took them away from him.

"Six thousand eight hundred and forty-three dollars," he read from the bill of sale. "I'll give you a draft on a San Antonio bank, Jeremiah. Thanks."

"You're welcome," Jeremiah said weakly. It was all he could say. He watched Kane write out the draft. Was this a mistake? He had brought into the valley a man who could pay for his own spread in cash. Had he set up still another independent ranchman who would turn against his benefactor?

"I'm making the draft for eight thousand, Jeremiah," Ed explained. "Put the balance to my credit here. I'll be needing saddles and things."

Good God, he had the money to buy anything he needed! Jeremiah was unhappier than ever. His owlish face twitched as Kane walked out of his office with a final nod and a last mocking grin.

TOMMY MCGEE was waiting outside, mounted on a swift, strong roan Ed had purchased from the livery stable. They would need more horses, but at the moment these two would suffice. For the present they needed to work more with their hands than on horseback—the house must be repaired, corrals mended and a barn thrown up behind the spring. Ed Kane had watched ranchmen store wild grass turned into hay by the mellowing sun and throw up watering troughs where a few head of choice cattle might drink in the dryest season and wondered why all men didn't do this. There was much to accomplish. He was impatient to get at it.

Tommy's horse was loaded heavily with supplies, enough for a long time, and they had to ride slowly. Kane wanted to ride this way, to approach his ranch from the back, to see whose cattle were running in the timber he had just purchased from Jeremiah Gilbert.

This road leap-frogging up the rim was the boundary line. To his right lay the Crown fences. It was common knowledge that Calhoun Conroy had thrown up fences on government land. It could be proved in court. But no man in the valley would cross the road with his herd and take advantage of the open country.

Once this had been the Carter Slade spread, the Crown foreman's father. The older Slade was a gentle and courteous man, long suffering before Conroy inroads, but never willing to give open battle. Carter coming after him was shrewd enough to realize that he could not combat the Crown alone. He had thrown in with them, working up until he was range foreman of the valley's top outfit, their equal in his own eyes if not in theirs.

And, at that moment, there came riding down the rim road the girl who had been largely responsible for Carter Slade's change of heart.

She was galloping her horse, scorning the danger

of loose rocks and twisting turns, but she slowed down to a walk when she saw the two men ahead of her. Ed gave her begrudging admiration. She could sit a horse more regally than any man he had ever seen, and the ride had brought high color to her cheeks, a redness to her lips and a flash to her eyes.

He tipped his hat, as did Tommy, and would have ridden by. But Catherine Conroy would not have it so.

"The Crown has used this road for a long time, Mister Kane," she said crisply. "I wouldn't advise you to make a habit of coming this way."

Seeing that she wanted to talk, if only to harangue, Kane nodded to Tommy to ride on. "This is a public road, Miss Conroy," he said politely. "I intend to use it whenever necessary."

Her cheeks flushed redder than ever. "Where do you think such an attitude will get you, Ed Kane?" she demanded, dropping the "mister." "Do you think my people will fold up and run like sheep because you are back?" Her glance roved to the guns at his side. "We are not afraid of those guns, Ed Kane," she said scornfully. "There is no killer Jeremiah Gilbert could hire who would frighten us."

Ed bit his lip. It made him wince to be called a killer. It made him angry to be called a Jeremiah Gilbert hireling. Everybody in the valley must think that of him. He must correct that impression.

"I owe Jeremiah nothing," he said curtly. "I paid cash for my land and for my cattle. I came back to the valley where I was born to live in peace, Miss Conroy. You carry that message to your father. I will return everything the Conroys send me with interest—including friendship."

They had ridden slowly and it was growing late. A thin cut of a moon hung low in the sky, silver-pale and shedding almost no light along the earth. The near-by forehead of Sunset Rim threw shimmering darkness over them, but it came and went in elusive shadows. The river was nearby, the wash of water over its shallow gravel bend a low murmur.

"Do you mean that, Ed Kane?" she asked after a long moment.

"I mean it," he answered firmly.

"Then why did you stand up with Tommy McGee? Why did you prevent our men from killing him—as he deserved?"

"Did he deserve it? Is a side of beef more valuable than a human life?"

"It is the principle," she said, tossing her head. Then, slumping forward in her saddle, "I'm tired of all this, Ed," she exclaimed. "This might as well be called the Valley of Hate. I remember you from when I was a girl, and how you used to tease me at dances. Yet now, simply because you are living in the valley across the road from us, I am told I should hate you, and must hate you."

"It isn't necessary," he insisted.

"There is nothing else," she snapped. Her voice was instantly aroused and he knew then how deeply she felt. The wild partisan instinct of her family governed her life also. "You have heard only one side of this valley feud, *their* side. It's impossible for me to trust you, or for anybody to trust you. Do you see why? Because, whatever you try to do, it will be for one side and against the other. You may not mean it that way, but you can't make a single move in the valley without helping either the Conroys or the Gilbert men. You stand between us and the government range up the valley, Mister Kane. That is why I cannot trust you."

He was a little piqued. "Did anyone ask you to?" he questioned sharply.

"No," she admitted, her head dropping again. "You didn't ask me to. But I wanted to, Ed Kane."

He was silent, all at once realizing how lonely she must be. She was twenty-four at least and all of her lifetime she had suffered from this valley hate. At dances only he and Carter Slade had "given her a rush." The others had danced with her politely, as a gesture, speaking with her stiffly, hailing the end of the set with sighs of relief. It was probable that never a single valley swain had ridden past the rim road and onto the broad veranda of Calhoun Conroy's house. Carter had gone, yes. Carter had gone and stayed as one of her father's men. But, knowing the pride that must be Catherine's, Ed gathered that she thought less of Carter for this, instead of more. Imperious people were always like that—hating those who will not yield, scorning those who will.

They heard hoofbeats in the dusk and out from the side rim road came a rider at a slow gallop. Even in the twilight they easily could recognize him as a Conroy, though Kane could not tell until he was right upon them that he was Davis Conroy, Calhoun's youngest son. It was like Calhoun, a man who had fought in the Civil War and had fled the South to escape Yankee rule, to name one son Jefferson and the other Davis.

"You had better go," Catherine said gently. "My brother won't like this."

Ed shook his head. He would not run. Let Davis Conroy make of this accidental meeting what he pleased.

Davis was a replica of his father and a counterpart of Jefferson, the older son—heavy, dark features, thick, sullen lips, dark eyes. He reined his horse and his angry gaze roved from Catherine to Ed and back again.

"You'd better come along," he said curtly, not challenging Kane directly.

Ed noticed something in the younger Conroy's left hand. It was wadded up tightly, but he recognized it for a lined sheet of tablet paper. For a moment he couldn't remember where he had seen it before, although the sight of it struck a responsive chord in his mind. Then he remembered. Mary McGee had affixed a note to a nail in his cabin. The note had said "I can't meet you anymore." So Davis Conroy had been the man who slipped away to meet Mary McGee in the deserted Kane cabin!

Kane's lips drew up in a straight, hard line. That was something else one could expect of an imperious haughty clan. Only the gentry women were good enough for them to meet in public, although they could not resist the allure of the other kind, and would steal away to meet them in darkness or support them in secrecy.

"It's a shame I'm reclaiming my cabin, Davis," he drawled. "Mebbe you had better build one of your own higher on the rim."

His insinuation was insulting and he meant it to be. Catherine could not decipher the hidden significance of his speech. She looked from one to the other in surprise. But Davis Conroy understood instantly. His dark face was suddenly drained of all color and his lank body actually trembled. His lips parted in a snarl and his right hand leaped down—

Before the gun was out of its holster he was looking into the barrel of an automatic.

"Don't be a damned fool," Kane said wearily. "You may be a Conroy but you can die like other men. The noble blood that flows through your veins doesn't make you bulletproof."

Davis Conroy was silent, but it was a raging

silence. "It is barely possible," Ed said slowly, biting off each word, "that I owe you an apology. I will take your word for it. Do I?"

This was unexpected. Davis Conroy could not answer for a moment. Catherine Conroy watched with growing amazement. None of this talk made sense to her. What manner of an apology could Ed Kane owe to her brother?

"You do," Davis said finally. There was something about his tone that convinced Kane of his sincerity.

Yet it was hard to say. This land had not yet learned the art of gentle apology. Ed Kane was more inexperienced than most. Never before had he been forced to make amends. No force compelled him now.

"Then I apologize, Davis," he said after a moment. "I made an insinuation without knowing anything of the facts or bothering to investigate. Furthermore, the matter was none of my business in the first place, and from here on I'll keep my eyes on my own range."

Catherine gasped. Never had she heard such talk from a man! This kind of placation could be expected from a Jeremiah Gilbert, but not from a man who a split second before could have shot her brother out of the saddle without danger of retribution—even the dead man's sister would have admitted that Ed had killed in self-defense. This apology, humble and complete, came from the lips of a man whose smoking death was a tradition as far as the Rio Grande and the Pecos, and even beyond.

Davis Conroy did not expect it either. That showed in his wide-open eyes, his parted mouth. Davis himself would never have said it, as no Conroy would have. A moment before, Davis had been vowing to himself that somewhere, and somehow, he would settle with Ed Kane.

But he had a gentleness that no other Conroy knew. Perhaps it came from his mother, who had died early in this harsh new land. He actually smiled.

"Thanks, Kane," he murmured.

"And no offense?" Ed questioned.

"Not at all," Davis said quickly. "In fact, quite the opposite. We must have a talk sometime."

"Good," Ed agreed.

He looked down at Catherine Conroy and chuckled at the wonder in her eyes.

"Buenos noches," he drawled, and spurred his horse down the side rim road.

Behind him Catherine regarded her brother in amazement. "Davis, what in the world?"

"Ask me no questions," he snapped, "and I'll tell you no lies."

THE CUMBERLANDS and the Winslows helped Kane comb the creek banks until all the longhorns were rounded up in the rebuilt branding pasture.

The two Winslow boys, Ellis and Carey, were typical of this country—tight-lipped but pleasant, never jocular but enjoying a light word. They sat around the campfire at night like Indians, always cautious and quick of movement, but never seemingly more than half awake. Matthew Cumberland and his boys were all of the hale and hearty type, bluff of manner and jovial of speech. The difference, Ed reflected, was in the background. The Winslows had built up slowly. Matthew Cumberland had come into the valley with a stake.

Three hundred and forty-two steers were brought out of the valley. Ed picked his hundred, regardless of the brand they wore, and worked with his neighbors to re-brand them his own Rolling R. The Winslows would have driven their remaining cattle off, but Kane would have none of it.

"The valley is all right," he said. Indeed the grass showed no depreciation. "Perhaps this valley can feed five hundred head. When you get to crowding me, I'll run your stuff across the creek and send it home."

This suited Matthew Cumberland. He boomed out a hearty assent. The Winslows were slower to accept. Indian blood flowed in their veins, but it was from a nester ancestor, rather than a Creek warrior, that they had inherited their suspiciousness. Traffic in skins and varmints had raised the Winslows above the level of the McGees—that and their quiet determination.

They rode away after two days and Kane turned his attention to the house and barn. McGee was not a good workman, having neither industry nor skill with tools. It seemed strange to Kane that anyone in a family could live in a country where sooner or later every man was dependent upon what he could build with his own hands out of makeshift implements without acquiring some skill with tools. All the McGees had been given employment by the valley ranchmen, only to be discharged as bad bargains.

But a change took place in Tommy. He was quieter, and did not grin as much. He tried hard, swinging a hammer until his hands bulged with blisters and his back ached at night. Toward Ed he displayed a dog-like devotion.

"You're giving me a chance, Mister Kane. You don't look at me like I'm a spotted hound pup."

"Don't call me 'mister'," Ed complained.

Tommy nodded but never adopted the use of the informal "Ed" or the masculine-like "Kane." Yet everybody else he hailed by his first name—even Matthew Cumberland, who was past fifty, and Jeremiah Gilbert, who rode out to inspect with sad eyes Kane's improvements.

"You're wasting time and money, Kane," snapped the banker. "You ought to be working your cattle and letting your house go until winter."

Ed grinned and did not argue. To Jeremiah anything that did not represent actual profit in dollars and cents was a waste of time.

For four days Ed and Tommy did not get away from the house. Then they rode through the valley to push their stragglers back toward the hills and to look for worm sores. This business of pushing the cattle up the heights was automatic. Leave the steers alone and they would stay down by the creek bank in the shade of the locusts and the scrub oaks, eating out the grass there while better grazing was available higher on the slopes.

Working down the valley, they came to the rim road. There they found forty head of Crown cattle grazing in a rich pocket softened and flushed by a wet-weather spring seeping out of the rocks.

Kane studied them grimly. Those cattle had not strayed over the road. For several hundred yards on the Crown side the terrain was rocky and uneven. No steer would go wandering across looking for better grazing beyond. And the country was not dry enough for the scent of water to carry that distance to them.

With a word to Tommy, he set the cattle in motion, driving them back across the rim, firing blanks into the air to whip them into a run.

Lumbering across the road, one of the ungainly creatures fell and fractured a leg on the treacherous boulders. It bawled in agony, looking up at Ed with appealing eyes. He shot it through the eyes.

"Come on, Tommy. Let's pull the carcass out of the road," he proposed.

At that moment Calhoun Conroy came riding down the rim road. He took in the situation with a glance of his flashing dark eyes.

"Who gave you permission to kill my cattle, Kane?" he demanded.

Ed was in no mood for apologetic explanations. "The same person who gave you permission to run steers on my land," he snapped back.

"That is government land on that side of the rim," Calhoun said coldly. "Steers will wander. The neighborly thing to do is to ask us to come and get 'em. We don't like other men to be driving our cattle."

His eyes flashed to McGee's perspiring face. "Especially riffraff who kill 'em for beef. Sure that wasn't what you had in mind with this steer, Kane?"

"Lemme handle him!" begged Tommy, pushing up before he could be stopped. His gun was half out of its holster before Ed could seize his shoulders and pull him back.

"We'll have no shooting here," Kane snapped.

"How much is the steer worth?" he demanded, turning to Conroy again. "I killed it to put it out of misery, but that doesn't matter before the law. I had no right to shoot it. Will fifty bucks cover it?"

"No steer is worth that much," growled Calhoun.

"Conroy stock must be," Kane said grimly, "with such blue blood around. I'll pay you fifty."

He pulled a bill out of his pocket and handed it to Conroy. The old man's face turned livid. He gasped a moment, then reached out and slapped the bill to the ground. Wheeling his horse, he galloped back toward his own ranch.

Ed picked up the bill with a cold smile.

4

TOMMY MCGEE'S HANDS were not meant for work. His fingers could fashion a cunning quail noose out of wild grape vines, but he could not use a hammer or a saw and he was almost helpless with a branding iron. After a week of hard effort, his enthusiasm waned and his old restlessness returned. With an apologetic grin he asked Ed for a few days off.

"I gotta get off by myself in the hills a couple of days, Mister Kane."

When Ed hesitated, thinking of the work that had to be done before the cabin was ready for occupancy, Tommy said quickly: "Oh, I figger you'll dock me for it, Mister Kane. I don't want you to pay me for nothing I don't do."

Ed sighed and consented. He understood what was driving Tommy away into the grayness of the upper rim. When a man was used to living alone, free and untamed, it was difficult to resign himself to daily toil. Tommy borrowed a side of bacon and a blanket and rode his small nimble horse up the cliffs behind the flowing creek.

Tommy McGee was a philosopher without knowing it. Here, high among the rocks, was his library. Below him stretched his laboratory table, and across it rode his subjects, for he could see from one end of the valley to the other, from the cedar clumps around Jeremiah Gilbert's unpainted ranch house to the tall cottonwoods standing guard over Calhoun Conroy's sprawling headquarters. What were only minute moving dots to the average eye were plainly recognizable characters to Tommy's overdeveloped vision. He knew them from miles above.

Tommy reached one of his favorite porches, tethered his horse and took a quail noose out of his saddlebag. It was an ingenious trap. Within an hour he had two birds dressed and cooking slowly over an improvised spit. He rolled a smoke and lay back against a rock ledge with a grunt of satisfaction. The charred remains of older fires showed that Tommy had camped here before. For years he had flitted in and out of these upper heights, bothering no one, never revealing what he saw, and seldom even speculating upon what happened below. Though the first stubble of manhood was new on his cheeks, Tommy McGee was already an old man in experience.

He was not bitter. Strangely enough, not a single

McGee was bitter. The entire family seemed reconciled to the sneers and the rebuffs of the valley. For years Sam McGee had eked out an existence on the ridges across from the Crown, moving from one range to another, throwing up board cabins when he could not find a deserted line-riding shack to occupy. The assortment of McGee children grew up in the same way, some dying young, some living on. Of the four who reached maturity, only three stayed in the valley—one a bartender, one a waitress and the valley's scarlet woman, the third a quiet, harmless wanderer of the ridges.

Sam and Miranda McGee now lived in a cabin across from the Crown watering holes and Tommy's mother augmented her husband's meager earnings by selling jams and preserves and making quilts for families like the Cumberlands and the Winslows. None of the three children ever visited his parents. Mary had been driven from home by an indignant father, who still read his Bible of an evening. What had happened to Mary did not concern Tommy. He did not bother to have beliefs on subjects that did not concern him. The relations of a woman and a man had never affected Tommy McGee. As the son of the only nester in the valley he could not be received as a suitor by any of the valley girls. There were never more than vague disturbances in the back of Tommy's brain when he looked upon young women. These he quickly stifled.

Tommy had been away from these hills too long. He smoked and looked and mulled over what had happened to him. It was hard to believe that he had actually challenged Carter Slade. He could shoot with a gun, perhaps better than any man in the valley, for he had downed quail on the wing and deer on the run. But, until that day of the trial, until he stepped out of the store knowing that Carter and the Crown men meant to kill him, he had never thought of using his gun against his fellow-man. Would he have killed Slade? Tommy shrugged his narrow shoulders. He probably would have. He probably still would.

His eyes turned to the southern end of the valley as he thought of Carter Slade and Calhoun Conroy. There a drove of men rode out from the Crown headquarters, spreading out in fan shape, working the brush along the creek bank. Though these men were miles away, Tommy knew each one. There was Carter Slade spurring his gray horse about. And Davis Conroy working for an hour and then riding away, disappearing into the brush behind the big twin boulders which marked the limits of the rapids where one of Tommy's brothers had drowned setting out trot lines for catfish.

Now Carter Slade was riding off. Going back up the rim, high and away from the ranch. Riding alone.

A speck flickered among the canebrakes by the creek's stills. Davis Conroy again, riding toward a

Crown line cabin in the cedars across the creek. The Crown seldom used this range, thick with cedar and canebrake. Tommy knew from experience that the cabin was crumbling and drafty.

His eyes came back to Bull Creek's mouth. Up the ridge Ed Kane was still working away. Then Tommy's eyes caught a flash of color among the scrub oaks. He chuckled. Catherine Conroy was riding across the plain toward the rim road. What would she do if she saw Kane?

Tommy did not think of Catherine Conroy as an attractive woman. He did not think of any woman that way. He thought of her only as the daughter of Calhoun Conroy, as haughty and as distasteful.

He saw her turn her horse off the road and ride to where Kane was working. Ed stopped digging, climbed out of the basin and rolled a smoke. They seemed to be talking friendly enough. Tommy shrugged his shoulders. This was beyond him. Why should Kane want to talk to Catherine Conroy?

His eyes wandered toward the sprawling heap that was Cotulla. Few people were stirring on the dusty streets. He saw a black dot crawling up the rim road. He had to strain his eyes to recognize his sister Mary. He regarded her with an indifferent gaze, wondering where she was riding to. But Mary was always riding off somewhere. She had to be back in town to serve supper at the hotel but her afternoons were her own.

She was riding a black horse which some admirer—one of the Cumberland boys, according to town gossip—had given her. Tommy shrugged his shoulders. He felt no resentment for Mary's reputation. She rode a mile up the rim road, then turned off into the cedars and started down the creek. Tommy raised his eyebrows. This would lead her into the canebrakes across the creek from the Conroy spread. Why would she want to ride there? Wild country. Few cattle trails.

His sharp ears caught the sound of hoofbeats and he froze against his rocky ledge and hoped that his horse grazing placidly in the hollow wouldn't give him away. A mount was an unusual luxury for Tommy. He began to wonder if it wasn't a nuisance also.

Who was riding this high on the rim? He raised his head cautiously over the ledge. A roan horse shot by him, no more than fifty yards away. Carter Slade!

Tommy reached for his gun. But Carter didn't see him. The Crown foreman was riding furiously along the top of the rim. Where was he going? There was a cattle trail over this rimtop. Tommy had stumbled upon it. It led over the heights to a mysterious somewhere that was beyond Tommy's comprehension. He had never gone out of the valley and never expected to. This wasn't a frequently traveled road. Most folks in the valley didn't even know about it. Carter rode down the trail a mile or more and then dipped into the high pines and scrub oaks back of the Cumberlands'.

Tommy frowned. Certainly Carter Slade wasn't paying social calls in this upper end of the valley!

Slade cut away from the trail from Gilbert's to the Winslows' and hugged the pines. Tommy's eyes lost him again and again in the tall timber. But the roan was a flash of light against a dark background and soon he saw Slade ride out of the pines behind Gilbert's house, fully five miles away. Now somebody was emerging from the Gilbert place and it wasn't Black Jim, the only rider Gilbert kept. Tommy squinted. Yes, Gilbert himself.

Tommy turned his attention to his roasting quail. Carter Slade had ridden cautiously along the higher edge of the rim and come into Gilbert's from downslope. The two men were talking out in the timber. He stored that fact away in the back of his mind. Many such items were thus catalogued. Tommy hadn't tried to add all of them up to arrive at a final sum and evaluation of the men and women he watched from a-high. This final process in philosophy was beyond his powers.

Having learned where Slade was going, and whom he wanted to talk to, Tommy turned his attention back to the valley. There, fully twelve miles from where Slade squatted talking to Gilbert, was the black speck that was his sister, riding now through deep canebrake. A mile or so below her was Davis Conroy, who had forded the creek and was coming slowly through the cedars. It occurred to Tommy that if each kept on his course they would meet just about at the rickety line cabin. As yet this made no impression on him.

Kane was still talking to Catherine Conroy at the basin. Tommy was slightly irritated with his employer. What could anybody find to talk about so long with a Conroy?

He turned his head farther south. Davis was riding up to the deserted line cabin and dismounting. Was squatting there smoking a cigarette. Mary came through the canebrakes and cedars. Davis helped her off the horse and kissed her. They disappeared into the cabin.

Tommy calmly continued to munch his quail. But a slow burning rage crept over him. He had known for years that the valley considered his sister a loose woman. That had not bothered him much. It seemed the fate of the McGees to be looked down upon, and if that hadn't been held against Mary something else would have. Tommy had never even thought of his sister's physical attractiveness. His life had been completely empty of sentimental relations, and thus he had no understanding of any such emotion.

Nor was he angry that Mary had ridden away into the woods to meet a man, and had gone into a cabin with that man. The rage he felt was all at Davis Conroy, the son of Calhoun Conroy and the colleague of Carter Slade. Tommy was puzzled to explain just what he did feel. Why should it matter to him at all? But he couldn't shrug it aside. His sister's conduct suddenly became a point of honor with him. It suddenly rankled. He and his people were ridge rats to the Conroys, to be sneered at in public, to be hauled into court over the killing of a yearling for beef. Yet one of them was good enough to be kissed by a Conroy, and to be carried into a deserted cabin by a Conroy.

Tommy let his fire go out. He smoked one cigarette after another, his eyebrows knit in perplexed thought. Finally he stamped out his fire, mounted his horse to ride into town.

It was sundown when he started down the rim. Below him he could see Carter Slade riding back across the rim road. And Mary galloping toward Cotulla. She would be late for supper at the hotel. Catherine Conroy's silk waist was a splash of color in the distance as she turned to the Crown. Davis Conroy splashed back across the creek.

Tommy spurred his horse faster. He rode down the steep road at a breakneck gallop. His young mouth was tight. His eyes glowed in the dusk like twin coals.

CARTER SLADE carefully awaited his time before speaking to Catherine Conroy, as he had intended for years to do. Ever since his boyhood days he had admired this tall, slim daughter of Calhoun Conroy, the valley's richest and most aloof man.

Somewhere in his teens Carter had changed in character from the smiling boy who rode these ridges with Ed Kane and Ellis Winslow, hunting antelope on the high slopes of the rim and black-tailed deer in the lush draws. The something that had happened to Carter Slade was the realization that his was a keener brain than other valley youngsters possessed, that he could engineer their movements and control their emotions by his capacity of leadership and command.

Perhaps with a different type of father, Carter might have grown into a different type of man. But the older Carter was a fussy person, of a nervous disposition, with a tendency toward fumbling incompetency. Work he did, harder than most ranchmen in the valley, but his was helter-skelter, disorganized labor. Before one task was finished he rushed on to the next, whining at the ill luck which constantly beset him.

Hard of hearing, he brooked no argument, not even from his broad-shouldered son, who knew more about the ranching business than he ever would and who, furthermore, possessed a gift of tying loose ends together and getting things done. Before Carter was twenty common talk over the valley asserted that the Slades' Double X would be better off if the young'un was running it instead of the old man.

Carter's mother died early—he hardly remembered her. Women too frequently died early in this land. Sarah Slade, humoring her husband's weaknesses, controlling his outbursts of temper, might have provided the maturing influence Carter Slade needed, the perspective that would have changed his personality.

Thus Carter in his teens was a schemer and a boy who worked undercover. He actually had no selfish purpose in mind. It was merely good business and grim necessity to persuade the older man to adopt sounder ranching practices without ever seeming to cross him. He must talk his father out of a cattle sale and into holding two-year-olds as stockers, without appearing to question his father's experience and wisdom. All the time he was consumed with a burning impatience. If the Double X were free of the old man's fumbling ways, it would grow by leaps and bounds. Once the old man passed on, Carter would take up the reins and challenge the Crown across the creek.

Thus for five years Carter waited impatiently for his father to die. Such years, naturally, affect a man's character and personality. They taught Carter patience, a cold, grim patience. They hardened his determination until it was like granite.

Perhaps he was always an unscrupulous type of youth. There is little way of knowing when unscrupulousness develops. At twenty-two Carter was owner of the Double X, which was mortgaged to Jeremiah Gilbert. The Slade ranch was next to the Conroys' Crown and Calhoun was pushing his steers across the creek in defiance of the Slade rights.

Carter could have fought. But he had learned as a boy the folly of open fight. Once he had talked Ed Kane into taking up a gun for him. Kane had never realized that, and would have thought little of it if he had. Carter never forgot the incident. It dawned upon him, despite his sixteen years, that it was better to have another man fight a battle than for oneself to fight.

Even in those teen years he considered marriage. A man must marry and raise children. The most attractive girl in the valley was Catherine Conroy. From his seventeenth year on, Carter Slade courted Catherine. When his father died, and the responsibility of the Double X was his alone, with the Crown pushing him back, he considered Catherine as an alternative to disputing Calhoun Conroy's march. For, if he were successful against Conroy's crowding, he still would lose Catherine.

He rode the rims also, though never as high as Tommy McGee, and never as peacefully. He looked down upon the Crown spread and coveted it. He admired old Calhoun, though he scorned the old Southerner's temper. He had some slight respect for Jefferson, the oldest son, though Jeff was as hot-tempered as his father without Calhoun's sober judgment. Davis he despised, and the feeling was returned with interest. The valley was waiting for old Calhoun to die and the Crown to fall apart, for nobody believed either son could carry it on. The valley joked that Catherine Conroy had more backbone and more brains than either of her brothers.

So Carter rode across the creek with his proposal to Calhoun Conroy. It was a humble proposal—on the surface. In return for a job, the Double X brand and corrals and claim to government grazing was the Crown's. Calhoun accepted quickly. He liked the young Slade boy. Not a drinking man. Hard worker. Good, solid business foundation. Carter became foreman and banked what Calhoun paid him. The Crown cattle pushed into the hills his parents had called home and Carter rode past their graves with Crown riders at his heels and felt no regrets.

Slowly but surely he worked himself up in the Crown organization. And he used still another method. Carter Slade had ridden the high rims and had found the pass through the hills right under Old Baldy's nose. He also had found another man willing to play a waiting game—Jeremiah Gilbert.

Gilbert and Slade could work together, when they wished. Carter was not willing to commit himself too far. He told Gilbert so frankly. If he could marry Catherine Conroy, he reasoned, the Crown would be his to rule and build, even if he must share the profits with Jefferson and Davis, who didn't deserve them. Although his suit was not received favorably, he was sure Catherine would, soon or late, accept him. Sunset Rim loomed high and forbidding on all sides. There was no crossing it for a daughter of Calhoun Conroy. And who else was there in the valley but Carter?

He had not intended to rush his proposal. He had learned well his lesson of patience, and the present situation was satisfactory to him. He was already worth more in solid cash than Calhoun Conroy, and he had cleverly seen to it that the Crown's financial status was none too secure. Catherine could take a year or ten to make up her mind. As long as old Calhoun lived, and trusted Carter's judgment, there was no point in calling for a showdown.

But now Ed Kane had come back to the valley. Carter had forgotten about Kane, retaining none of the memories of youthful friendship that had thrilled Ed when the former Ranger looked into Carter's face and shook hands. What Carter thought of when he met Kane in the hotel was the possible challenge to his plans. For he recalled, with that queer, quick, letter-perfect memory of his, that Catherine had always smiled upon Ed at dances and rodeos and that Ed's father and mother had been the only people in the valley with whom the Conroys had been sociable.

Carter knew the men in the valley, knew how far he could trust them, how far he could go with them. He feared none of them but Jeremiah, and for the moment he played his game with Jeremiah, and hoped that a disastrous showdown could be averted. The Winslows, the Cumberlands and the Merricks were good, down-to-earth people who kept within the shadow of their own corrals and did no more than mutter about the dribble of cattle out of their grasslands. Carter and Jeremiah kept it that way—a mere dribble. Any more would arouse suspicion. Neither was in a position to account for a notable increase in either herds or bank account. Both were patient men.

But Kane? Here was a man who had ridden away to become a legend with the Rangers. Here was a man who was quite likely to ride up the rim to see what was on the other side, and to wonder at a cattle trail which appeared by magic in the midst of the passes and led away to the rimtop. Jealously Carter guarded his rimtop secret. It was that which led him to file charges against Tommy McGee. He had seen Tommy slipping among the boulders and crevices and wanted the nester out of the way.

Arousing Calhoun Conroy's anger was easy. Carter could always handle him like that—by appealing to his fierce Southern pride.

Such means could also be used with Catherine.

He rode after her as she left the house on her gelding. For days, ever since Kane's return, he had awaited this opportunity.

"Mind if I mosey along with you?" he smiled.

"Of course not," Catherine said readily.

She had never attempted to diagnose her feelings for this square-jawed, sharp-eyed man who was such a vital influence at the Crown. She admired Carter for his judgment and his dogged energy, as did the other Conroys. Neither Davis nor Jefferson was jealous of Carter's efficiency, although the former made no effort to conceal his dislike for the Crown foreman and frequently would not sit in the same room with him.

Carter rode a long way in silence. It was difficult to begin such a conversation. He regretted that he hadn't spent more time with her in just idle chit-chat, complimenting her upon her eyes and hair and such talk as that. Had he foreseen a necessity to press his case so swiftly, he would have mapped out a clever, careful campaign, and pursued it attentively. But the years had slipped up on him. He had been too busy with the Crown business—and his own. With no rival in sight, he had taken her eventual consent too much for granted.

"Catherine, I'm not an eloquent man," he said slowly. Carter Slade was not unaware of his ability at speech-making. He was not a screaming, ranting orator such as spoke in Cotulla on the Fourth of July, but he could say what was on his own mind in words chosen to strike a responsive chord among his listeners. "I work too hard. I've spent too much time in these past few years worrying about the Crown's business, and—not enough about the Crown's daughter."

He thought that a pretty phrase. He paused to watch its effect. Catherine merely raised her eyebrows.

"My heart and soul are in the Crown," he continued. "For two reasons. First, I'm that type of man. Second, for a long time I've thought of the Crown as something that would someday belong to me—in part, at least."

Catherine slowed down her horse and studied his serious face. What was the man talking about, anyhow?

"You were the cause of that, Catherine," Carter said with forced gentleness. "For years now I've thought of—dreamed of—the day you would be—my wife."

There, he had said it. And rather gracefully too, he thought. He waited for her to answer.

The girl's eyebrows were knit into question marks. Was this dark-faced man actually proposing to her? She studied his face again. Yes, that was it!

It was the first proposal Catherine Conroy had ever received. She was twenty-four and she had been a lovely girl all her life, with background and money and physical charm, but this was her first experience of that kind. There might have been others had she ever provided an opportunity. She was thrilled with it, yet she was disappointed. How matter-of-fact Carter was, and how poor his efforts to act otherwise! Her lips tightened. It was as if he had studied her teeth and forelegs and had considered her good breeding stock for his range!

Yet—he was serious. She caught back the words that started to leap from her lips. She was sure Carter Slade had never proposed to another woman. She was sure also that Carter loved her—as he understood love. Carter would have been shocked to know that Catherine Conroy sensed his character far better than did her father or brothers. Some things she did not suspect him of, and would not believe if she were told. But she knew of his will to possess and to hold and of his willingness to sacrifice and wait to attain.

"I'm sorry, Carter," she smiled. "If I had seen you throw your loop, I would have stopped you."

His eyelids flickered. He had not expected this. He had been prepared for a "I can't make up my mind," or "Isn't this rather sudden?" or a "Carter, I can't believe it!" He would have been astonished if Catherine had accepted him immediately and melted into his arms like a flurry of snow. He knew she wasn't that type and he didn't consider that she held him in that much affection. But her casualness! And firmness!

"Perhaps I should have expected this, Carter," she was saying thoughtfully. "If so, I'm sorry. I didn't. If I had, I could have given you a hint, and kept you from having to say it. I will never marry you, Carter. I will never think of it seriously. You're not what I want for a husband."

There! She had said it as gently as she could

without hiding the emphasis of her refusal. She didn't want to hide that. Catherine Conroy was as direct as her dark-eyed father.

"I see," he mused.

"We'll forget you said it, Carter," she smiled, holding out her gloved hand. "I'm turning off here. You're going on to town, I suppose."

"Yes, on to town," he muttered.

She pressed his hand, then touched spurs to her gelding and went loping down the rim road, turning off into the pines near the creek. Carter looked after her with dull, unbelieving eyes. He wasn't prepared for such a refusal. Ordinarily he wasn't the type of a man to take a first no, but he couldn't accept her attitude as anything but a final dismissal of his case.

5

DAVIS CONROY HAD his family's harsh face, but not their eyes. As Mary dismounted, he caught her in his arms with a smile that had none of the Conroy hauteur. She returned his kiss, then pushed him back.

"Davis, this mustn't happen again!" she gasped.

"You can stop it anytime you like," he reminded her. "All you have to do is say the word."

"You know I can't marry you, Davis. We won't argue about that anymore."

He pulled her into the cabin. It was only ten feet

square and part of the roof was caving in. But since Ed Kane had returned, it was the only safe spot he knew.

"I was afraid you wouldn't get my note," he grinned. "Look, honey, don't beat around the bush with me anymore. If you love me, forget all this valley feuding and let's go hunting a parson."

It seemed unbelievable that, as boyish and as informal as he was, he could be Calhoun Conroy's son.

Mary shook her head. "No, Davis. You're used to plenty. It's easy to talk about turning your back on your family, but you can't do it. I can't even shake the specter of mine."

"Try me and see," he urged.

He pulled away from her. "It isn't only you, Mary," he said grimly. "I'm sick of the whole damned business. We're the Conroys—we must ride with our heads in the air. We can't mix with hands and ordinary people. Everybody around us is our enemy. They are jealous of us and are just looking for a chance to pull us down. I don't believe that, Mary. I think if we gave people a halfway chance, they would like us—well, some of us."

"You perhaps," Mary said tenderly. "And Catherine. Your father and Jefferson—never."

"I guess not," he sighed. He reached for her again.

"What are we going to do, honey? I'm not going to let you go, quit even talking about it. I'll marry you and stay here and face it, or we'll run off."

"The past would always follow us. I have too much to look back upon, Davis."

"Your family—I don't give a hoot in hell about your family!"

"It's not my family," she answered gently. "I think I could forget about them, too. But there were other men, Davis. I was young and I was a McGee and I didn't see anything else for me. If I had known you then as I do now—"

"Isn't that my business?" he asked harshly.

"Could you face the taunts of—men I've known? Think how it would tickle them. You a Conroy. Sure, they know the wife of Davis Conroy. She used to be Mary McGee, a waitress. And worse."

"I could jam their words down their throats," he said hotly.

"And there would be more feuding," she said gently. "You would shoot a Winslow or a Cumberland and they would team up against the Conroys. Then your people, though they hated me, would help you. No, Davis. This is the last time I'm going to meet you."

"You mean that, don't you?" he whispered.

"I do."

She sat down on the crude bunk. It was hard to believe that Mary McGee, despite her way of living, could grow prettier with each passing year.

But she did. She was now in the full glory of womanhood. Davis eyed her hungrily. It was easy to see why other men itched to possess her.

"Our last time, Davis," she smiled at him, taking his hand. "Hurry. Let's make the most of it."

A sound in his throat was not unlike a sob. He reached for her with hungry arms.

ED KANE was putting in the last touches to his dam. He changed the course of his spring temporarily and piled rocks waist high across the old channel. Now he was tamping in clay brought from the creek banks, mixing it with bluestem into a crude but serviceable, and endurable, mortar. It was drying rapidly in the hot sun. By afternoon he could shovel dirt and gravel into the temporary basin and let the dam hold back the spring water until the basin was filled. This would be strong enough to withstand an overflow.

Engrossed in his work, he did not hear Catherine's horse. He was not aware of her presence until she said, close enough to startle him:

"Haven't you time for company?"

He jumped to his feet. For a moment he was embarrassed. Then he grinned.

"What do you mean sneaking up on a man like a hungry wildcat?"

"I am hungry," she admitted. "Hungry for talk."

She sat down under the shade of a hackberry. Her white silk blouse was cut low enough to show the gentle swell of her bosom and her dark hair was done up in a gaily colored scarf. Her riding skirt was of doeskin. As she swept her feet in under it, Ed caught a flash of bare flesh. But she didn't seem ashamed. She smiled up at him, as he joined her under the hackberry and rolled a smoke.

"I'm sorry I was so unpleasant the other day," she said sweetly. He could remember that about Catherine Conroy—the sudden changes from storm to sweetness. "But my family is upset that you came back. They figure on running cattle on this benchland this winter."

"It was my dad's place," he said a little shortly. "I'm just working to the river. I won't bother the Crown if the Crown doesn't bother me."

"I'm glad to know that, Ed," she sighed. "Everybody else hates us so."

"Shouldn't they? Nobody likes to be strong-armed."

"Isn't it necessary?" she demanded. "Doesn't every ranch take in all the grass it can? We're no different from any other outfit. We want more cattle and more grass. The men up the valley want the same thing. So do you, Ed Kane. You bought timberland back of here your father never owned. Why don't you just stay on the benchland, as he did? You know why Jeremiah Gilbert sold it to you."

"Yes, I know why," he admitted after a moment.

"Jeremiah Gilbert wants me here. He thinks the Crown is afraid to start pushing me around."

"Exactly," she said scornfully. "And the Crown isn't afraid. You know that, Ed. Or do you?"

"I know it," he admitted with another shrug. "But make no mistake about it, Miss Conroy. I'm here to stay."

"Maybe," she snapped.

Then her mood changed. "But why did you bring that up? I came over here for pleasure, not to start a row."

"Pleasure?"

"Yes."

There was unconscious coquetry in her smile. Catherine Conroy, daughter of Calhoun Conroy, had never been afforded an opportunity to be coquettish. The men she had known, except Carter Slade, were men who opposed her father and her brothers. To be friendly with them, much more coquettish, meant sacrificing her family's pride. She was too much like her father to consent to that.

"I was lonesome," she explained. "Davis is down in the lower flat. Jeff and Father are trading cattle in town. And Carter is off somewhere."

"And I'm the last resort," he grinned. "Thanks."

Her blue eyes studied his face. He had never experienced such a frank gaze—from her kind of woman.

"Yes, you're the last resort," she agreed. "If you don't turn out to be sociable and friendly, I guess

I'll live and die in this valley without ever having known a friend. A true friend."

Her loneliness and heartbreak were evident. He studied her flushed face, and noticed again the roundness of her body and the gracefulness of her long legs. A pretty girl, a beautiful girl. He had seen men killed over women not nearly so physically attractive. Yet here, in this small, grim valley, under the shadow of towering Sunset Rim, she was a virtual prisoner.

"I hope to be friends with all the Conroys," Kane said gently. "Especially with you."

"You always did make pretty speeches like that," she said, with a lazy grin.

Now she was lying back against the tree with her hands folded under her head for a pillow.

"I mean it," he insisted. "If you could get your family to come down off its high horse, we could even work together. I'm no Jeremiah Gilbert man, Catherine. I'm my own master. I paid for my land and my stock in cash. I promise you that the Crown will start anything that starts."

"Ed, I'm glad to hear that! It hurt me when you came back—and I heard Jeremiah Gilbert was setting you up on this benchland so you could stop the Crown moving up the valley."

"It isn't so."

"I'm glad," she repeated. She looked off. "I don't have pleasant memories, Ed. Life wasn't pleasant as a girl, and it isn't pleasant now. I don't remember liking many people. Most of them I was afraid to like—they were an enemy before I ever knew them. But Carter—and you . . .”

Now she was leaning back against the hackberry, and the gracefulness of her slim body was more evident. Ed Kane, who had seen San Antonio and Juarez, smiled at her pose. He must credit her with innocence, yet he had never seen a charmer, professional or otherwise, so quick to utilize a background—and a mood.

She continued to look away. Apparently she was busy with her own thoughts. He was willing for it to be that way—he also was engrossed in his. He was thinking back to other days when she had worn pigtails and had recited “Evangeline” in school. She was a smart child. Older than she, he had known that the Cotulla school teachers were compelled, for the sake of harmony, to lower Catherine Conroy’s grades and at the same time mark up her classmates, June Winslow and Cora Cumberland and Phyllis Merrick. It was a little thing. He grinned at his remembering it. Yet it was typical.

He was not to blame that he had never looked at her as a woman before. He could remember also, from away back, that she was a creature of moods, at times a little hellcat, at other times the personification of feminine sweetness. She chose to be that now. Had she been another person, he would have wondered if she were not trying to flirt with him. He wondered anyhow.

And yet, as he wondered, he knew the answer. She would never stoop to artifice. Girls in this valley did, when they were very young and first feeling the sensation of looking upon a boy as other than a dirty-fingered, clumsy nuisance. But that didn't last long. Kane, who knew more of the outside world than Catherine, had long ago realized the cause for what preachers loved to call this new land's moral primness. They were no more moral than Easterners. It was simply that romance, illicit or otherwise, had such a short time to live. The lives of men and women were so different. One was on horseback, one in the kitchen. A boy was in the saddle at sixteen, a girl in the kitchen as young, if not sooner. No common meeting ground could be found for fugitive passions.

A woman, like a maverick, must be branded on the run. The same weapon was used to uphold respect for a wedding ring as for a calf's brand. If anything, retribution came quicker and sterner.

And, necessarily, as often the wrong woman was branded. The men could accept it philosophically. There would be many instances this spring when bawling offsprings of Kane's cows would be caught up by Crown riders or Jed Cumberland's crew and branded falsely. But, in the long run, it would even up. When Kane found a motherless calf in his brakes he would slap his iron upon it. Because a wrong brand was found on a dogie was no sign of guilt—unless a brand had been changed.

To the dogie, it made little or no difference. Grass was grass and water was water, and one branding iron hurt as badly as the next. But to women, also swept up in the same impersonal rush, it must be different.

Here was a maverick unbranded. Her eyes came back to Kane's and something in his look caused her to blush.

Her flushed cheeks and her trembling body caused Kane to act in a way he had neither anticipated nor desired.

He seized her roughly and pressed his lips against hers.

For a moment there was the thrill of her response, rushing up from inside her in a flow she could not have checked if she had tried. And, for the moment, she did not choose to try.

But even as he pressed her closer, Kane realized theirs was an impersonal kiss. Even while his arm tightened around her body he knew that this was a gesture neither of them could interpret—except in a vein neither of them wished to admit.

Suddenly she stiffened. He had expected it. He was only surprised that it had not come sooner. She pushed him away. For a fleeting second he held. He could have held longer. That brief opposition to her wishes infuriated her. She scratched his face in a sudden motion. Blood dripped from one cheek as he stepped up and back.

She was furious. Her eyes were dark, flashing

pools of fire. "How dare you, Ed Kane!" she whispered hoarsely. "If I had a gun I would kill you."

She was berating a man of gentle philosophy, but of a stern will and a certain stubbornness he had never been able to explain himself. It was the same stubbornness that had sent him walking across the Cotulla street to stand at Tommy McGee's side. In many ways Ed Kane was more civilized than the country in which he lived. In certain queer ways he was wilder than it had ever been.

With women he had always been gentle—before this. Men are always at an extreme with women. Either women are china dolls that may crush within rough fingers or they are soulless creatures for but one purpose—a man's pleasure.

Women have never learned that. Women can never understand that a word from them, or a gesture, can change a man from one viewpoint to the other. When this transition comes, rushing up in a flow of words either unreasonably harsh or cloyingly sweet, they think a man has changed. So they mourn the loss of the other man—which was probably the one they wanted.

It was not Ed Kane's way to show his temper by impetuous words or by swift action. The blood beating against his temples was hot and bitter—perhaps under a microscope it would have been jet black in color. But his lean face was impassive and his mouth crooked in a mirthless grin.

"Isn't that what you came here for?" he asked.

A man has that power which women seldom possess—to choose the one word, the one gesture, that will hurt the other the most. Had he scratched her in return, or slapped her, she would have stormed a moment and then been quick to arbitrate, to admit herself as much to blame as he. Catherine Conroy, who had lived with men, would probably have held out a hand in a masculine gesture of atonement.

But he had charged her with what any woman would resent, even the women who would have been guilty for cheaper reasons than Catherine ever found necessary.

The anger faded. In its place came a sob, then open tears. She flung herself on her gelding and before he could believe his eyes she was galloping through the brush, back to the Crown.

A man always has such action in his favor. It is an advantage that the ways, and the beliefs, of the world have never let a woman overcome. He can call her a name, even in insinuation, that crumples down any defense she might have, leaving her no choice but flight.

There is no word of similar purport that can be hurled back in return. Women, sneeringly accused of doing most of the talking, can always be outtalked.

The hurt, at the time, seems to be all against the woman. But when such words are used, a man is never sure that he is right. Even if wordly evidence accumulates to support him, his own vanity will not permit him to be sure. And the uncertainty hangs on until, in the end, the man is more gravely wounded by his own speech than the woman. Then he must, at any cost, see if his judgment has been premature.

6

CARTER RODE BACK to where his men were working cattle. Davis had already left, but the comings and goings of the two Conroy sons never upset the routine of the Crown ranch. At first, Calhoun Conroy was the overseer, never participating in the branding and worming, but sitting apart on his black horse and watching with cold, disdainful eyes. Then Carter Slade took over. The hands liked him better. In the first place, he worked himself. In the second, he unquestionably knew his cattle.

"Work the lower ridge," Carter told Squinty Cox, "and then ride the upper pasture for strays."

His face was dark with fury. Catherine's cold rejection of his suit settled the indecision that had been his for two years now. His future lay with Jeremiah Gilbert. Perhaps the high and mighty Conroys, secure in their belief that theirs was a superior blood and all other men were beneath them, thought he would go on being a hired hand.

But they were wrong. Long ago he had decided that, one way or another, the Crown would be his.

He left his crew and rode straight up the rim. As soon as he was high enough to be hidden from any curious gaze from below, he turned up the valley and rode along the high ledges. Here was rocky land unfit for grazing—only in the first days of a wet spring did Crown cattle come this high. This was his secret highway along the outskirts of the valley. He could ride it undetected and look down upon the valley beneath him and think out his plans. For years he had thought about them patiently, holding back the day he would tip his hand, rather dreading it.

This high hidden ground made possible his pact with Jeremiah Gilbert. Theirs was a mildly profitable relation. Strange to say, Carter was forced to hold Gilbert back—the banker wanted to push their nefarious trade for more than it could stand. If too many cattle disappeared up the rimtop there would be concerted action by the valley men to find just who was carrying off their beef and how. Carter did not want that. They could, he told Gilbert, afford to be patient.

They were making money. Even after paying Black Ben and the two men who slipped across the rimtop to take over the steers, they were making money. A thousand head of beef a year brought in at least twenty grand to split between them. Carter had his sacked away in Jeremiah's bank. No one else knew about it. Calhoun Conroy would have been astounded to learn that his foreman had more solid cash to his credit than the Crown.

He was to meet Jeremiah Gilbert this afternoon. Gilbert kept him posted as to affairs of other ranches—the Winslows and the Cumberlands, the Merricks and the Hillhouses. It was about time for Winslow to start rounding up his stock across the creek. Jeremiah, who owned these men body and soul, always advised them when to start bringing in their beef. A day or so beforehand, word was gotten to Carter, who in turn passed it along to Black Ben, who sent his two men down the slopes. It was a sweet setup. Carter mused as he rode toward Jeremiah's that there would be no need to change it even after he had taken the Crown for his own.

Gilbert met him a few hundred yards back of the sprawling shack that served as his ranch headquarters. Squatting amid the pines, without a fire and with only the smoke from Carter's cigar as a giveway, they thought themselves hidden from all eyes. So they were—except from Tommy McGee's.

"I'm ready to crack down on the Crown," Carter said curtly. "I've had all I can stand over there."

Jeremiah nodded. Carter himself had delayed this showdown fight. Two years ago Jeremiah believed he was ready for it. Resentment was hot against the Conroy clan. He believed that at a signal from him all the valley men would gather to ride against the Crown.

"This Kane ain't working out like I wanted," Jeremiah mumbled. "He could pay his own freight. And he ain't anxious to mix it with the Crown men."

"Kane is dangerous," Carter snapped. "I've thought of how to get him out of the way. He's on land the Crown has used before. I can work old Calhoun up to burning him out. Mebbe we'll get Kane in the process. That wouldn't hurt. I don't trust him."

Carter should have said he was afraid of Ed Kane. He was. He didn't like his old friend's calm, clear gaze. Kane was too unruffled. And too entirely natural.

Gilbert picked his discolored teeth with a sharp twig. "You got a heap of gun-slicks over there. That Purdy, for instance."

"I'll have 'em up the rim when you wanna raid the Conroys," shrugged Carter. "Old Calhoun and the boys don't ever ride with us anymore. We got to work the lower country soon anyhow. That'll be a good time."

"Suits me," Jeremiah said laconically. But his sharp, piggish eyes gleamed with enthusiasm.

Carter knew what he was thinking. Soon the Crown and the lower end of the valley would be under his thumb. Slade had no intentions of reminding Gilbert this prematurely that he had the cash to operate the Crown himself, and wouldn't need or tolerate the banker's support. That could wait until later, when he had Gilbert in the hollow of his hand.

"Everything is government land except the homestead," mused Carter. "If that's burned out, I can probably pick up the corrals and barns for little or nothing. Then I can dicker with the girl for the cattle."

Jeremiah nodded. This was all talk that had passed between them many times. His sharp eyes studied Carter's face. He wasn't as dumb as Slade thought. Evidently Carter wasn't going to get the girl. He had guessed, shrewdly, for Carter had never dropped a hint, that this was what held up Slade's action.

"I told Black Ben to work on Kane," Carter confided. "After this year he'll probably be begging you for a loan, like the rest of 'em."

Jeremiah bared his unkept teeth. "Tell Ben to rush him."

"Better not go too fast," warned Carter. "Remember, Kane was in the Rangers."

"No man is smart enough to see through this setup," shrugged the banker. "It's fool proof."

"I don't know about that."

Jeremiah stood up. "Get old Calhoun after Kane. As soon as you burn him out, carry the boys down the valley. We'll pay the Crown a little visit while you're gone."

"Good," Carter grinned. He climbed onto his horse. "I'll mosey on," he said.

Jeremiah looked after him with glittering eyes. He could see through Carter Slade. Slade had been all set to double-cross him if Catherine Conroy had taken him up. Now, rejected by the Conroy girl, he was ready to play Jeremiah's game. But at the first chance, he would get off the trail. He was holding back something. What? Jeremiah had to study all the angles.

Jeremiah never could trust any man. Like any wise general, Jeremiah always mapped out his path of retreat before he charged to the attack. Carter Slade might just possibly get too big for his breeches. Just possibly.

Carter rode slowly back along the upper rim. He had not wanted it this way. Over and above his desire to possess the Crown, and to rule as cattle lord of the valley, he wanted to marry Catherine. Even such a cold, analytical man must have his lonely longings for a woman. The fact that they were rarer in Carter's nature than with most men, and more easily curbed, did not make them any less acute. Catherine was more desirable physically to Carter than to Ed Kane, but it was Carter's nature to suppress any desire that did not impress him as practical, or did not further his own ends.

Even as he plotted his treachery to the Conroys, he wondered how he might yet have her. It was in his nature, when once rebuffed, to consider force as the only other alternative. Persuasive powers were his to a greater extent than he realized, but he did not believe in them except in isolated instances. As a broad, grand strategy, he had never seen them work.

Perhaps, her father killed, her brothers shot down, her ranch in his hands, she would reconsider. Again Carter Slade was guilty of comparing the hearts and the desires of others to his own. His viewpoint was narrow because he had glutted himself on ambition and desire and had never given it a chance to grow. The man who ruled over the valley's grazing lands must be the valley's most desirable man, regardless of his appearance, his personality or even his color. It would be so to Carter.

He was judging Catherine by what she seemed on the surface. And, indeed, the surface was all that ever interested Carter. To be happy, she required power and money and envy from others. That was the only side of her he had ever seen, for Catherine had never come to him as he worked on a springbank, and never had sat against a hackberry trunk with a far-off look in her eyes.

He was in no hurry. He had many things to think about. At times he regretted his association with Jeremiah because he was afraid of Gilbert's rashness. What made Carter effective, and dangerous, was his patience. Even if there had not been Catherine to consider, he would have restrained

Gilbert in the little man's almost fanatical desire to crush the Crown.

While he held Calhoun Conroy and the two Conroy boys in some contempt, because they permitted their overbearing natures to interfere with their business judgment, he was also well aware that the Conroy fighting spirit had not died out, but had been passed on to at least one son, Jefferson, and perhaps to Davis as well. Davis did not carry a chip on his shoulder as the old man openly boasted of doing, but the youngest Conroy could shoot and ride and Carter, who never liked to overlook any factor, did not intend to dismiss him as harmless.

He took another cigar from his leather case and bit off the tip. When he raised his eyes again, they narrowed into twin pin points. He was almost at the peak of the rim now. Below him, to one side, was the hidden pass through which Black Ben and his fellow rustler drove valley cattle. This trail Carter thought unsuspected by valley men, who always hunted for rustler trails to the south, believing no steer could be driven up Sunset Rim's steep, forbidding side.

A man was bending over examining hoofprints in the trail! Carter recognized the man as Ed Kane—and cursed.

For a second Slade forgot his usual caution. He threw his rifle to his shoulder and fired twice before he realized Kane was out of range and, moreover, that downhill shooting was usually ineffective.

Kane darted for the shelter of the brush, whipping out a pistol. Carter touched spurs to his horse and galloped away. This was no fight of his; and he cursed at hurriedly firing the two shots. Now Kane would be sure that this high-rim trail demanded his investigation. Knowing Kane, he could not be too sure of the outcome. Beyond the rim Black Ben kept a close watch. Black Ben was a man like Slade in many respects—patient and cautious, determined not to make the mistakes which had sent other rustlers dangling off into empty space. But Carter did not sell Kane short.

Perhaps, as it was growing dark, Kane would turn back to his ranch and abandon his trailing until another day.

Carter hoped so. In any event, Jeremiah was right; they must move hurriedly, and boldly, against Ed Kane.

ED KANE finished his dam by mid-afternoon. He rolled a smoke, squatted and watched with satisfaction as the spring water teeming into the basin began to clear. Within a day's time here would be a waist-deep pool of spring water which would satisfy the thirst of more cattle than he could ever run in this upper flat.

He stamped out the cigarette and thoughtfully studied the terrain about him. His father had chosen this homestead because of its available water, but not even Henry Kane had visualized what Ed was planning—several overflows from this natural basin instead of one, water tricklets spreading into the bluestem on either side of the bench, creating a dozen lush flats where only one had existed before.

Kane smiled at his own perspicacity. Two weeks before he would have scoffed at the idea that he would become enthusiastic over working his own range—even to running the stock, much less throwing up rock dams with his own hands and planning overflow ditches that would give him a few additional acres of dry weather grass.

What had caused this change in him? Meditating upon it, he recalled his conversation with Catherine Conroy and saw again the queer deep pools that were her eyes and felt once more the rounded firmness of her body that she exposed even more carelessly than Mary McGee ever would dare. Ed Kane had talked to, and had thought of, two women since returning to the valley. He had also thought of, in the same impersonal way of thinking with which he had planned his dam and his overflow ditches, the advantages and the necessity of his marrying.

It was nothing new for Ed Kane to consider marriage. He was not without appreciation of what a woman meant, either spiritually or physically. But he had a softness, as far as women were concerned, that was out of tune with this new land where thoughtfulness was not always possible or convenient. Riding along trails alone, brooding over secret campfires, he had reflected much about his mother and what her life had been, and why she had died before fulfillment of her life and what life would have been for him had she lived.

The trails he had ridden away from Sunset Rim had given Ed Kane a media of comparison and contrast which no other man in this valley could know. Fairness and consideration for others, friends or strangers, was as much a part of Kane's makeup as the wrinkles under his gray eyes. He had seen enough harshness to dislike it, particularly toward women. He had lived without women on womanless trails long enough to realize that men shifted burdens and responsibilities onto women's shoulders without bothering to estimate either a fair proportion or the inevitable result.

There would be a woman in the house he would build on the benchland. As yet she was a vague, indistinct shape, like the trickles of water pouring off into the sun-parched thickets. There would be children, and their lives would not be harsh and grim as his had been, but of a more even tenor, with an accent on laughter rather than stark necessity.

Kane wondered if he would ever experience again the same wild sweet sentiment he had felt for the daughter of an Army officer at Fort Clark. That had been love as he was brought up to think of love—something queer and inexplicable, something fleeting and momentary, if not actually unattainable. That type of love, he knew, was not for his type of man, if it was for any type. No woman's smile or eyes or body could make up for what many women lacked, or satisfy all the desires that a man felt.

For years he had mourned the flaxen-haired girl at Fort Clark. Now, riding slowly along the rim of the benchland, he was glad she was not with him and that he was free in heart and mind to ponder upon, and eventually seek out, the woman who did belong here, who would be as much a part of the earth as had been his mother who now lay beneath it.

Ed Kane had eyes that were restless both by nature and by training. A hoofprint that another man would not have seen presented a challenge to him. He saw one now. Without leaving his saddle, he knew it had not been made by Tommy or himself.

He frowned at his own suspicions. That chapter in his life must be thrust behind him. He must cease to regard each unexplained hoofprint as a menace to his existence and a challenge to his sense of duty.

But a man who had spent years following faint hoofprints cannot shake the habit at once. Ed Kane followed the mysterious rider's trail to the creek bank and noticed, without immediately forming an opinion, that five steers had crossed the creek there, either shortly before or after the unknown rider.

More than likely they were his own cattle. It was not often that the Winslow or Cumberland beef strayed this far up the river. He swung back into his saddle and splashed across the rippling Frio.

This was government land, but it was pasture used more often by the Crown than by any of the upper valley people. He noticed with quickening interest that the five steers were leaving a close trail, as if they had been driven. But not until another rider joined the first behind the cattle prints did he decide that here was something which demanded his quick investigation.

The trail led up the ridge away from the rim road, which confirmed Kane's impression that the steers had not merely roamed. Here was rocky terrain and now the trail was so faint that only an expert could follow it: Here were tiers of rock ridges that no man in the valley wanted or would ever want—a gnarled, twisted stretch of hilly country taken over by scrub cedars and forgotten by valley men who shrugged it off as wasteland. Once, Kane remembered, a rustler had escaped into these ridges and had held out for days against a manhunt in which every outfit in the valley had taken part.

Probably this could be called Crown land, yet the Crown never used it. Kane watched carefully for a sudden turning in the trail that would throw guilt upon some valley spread. For certainly this cattle path could not lead up the steep side of Sunset Rim. Even now Kane's horse was picking a slow, careful progress along slippery shelves. There were marks to show that here a cow had rolled off its feet, and had been prodded up.

Kane stopped to rest his horse and roll another cigarette. He had made a new discovery—other narrow trails were filtering into this one.

Ahead of him, now in plain sight, was a gap in the grim face of Sunset Rim that hinted at a pass he had never found, or had never heard valley men speak of. All his life he had thought of Sunset Rim as completely shutting off the valley on two sides.

But he knew, from his years with the Rangers, that rustlers have a genius for ferreting out lost passes and for moving stolen cattle along cliffsides that would dismay an honest ranchman. Too many trails came into this one path for it to be coincidence. There, lurching drunkenly along the side of the rim, was a path from the lower valley, over which Crown cattle had probably been driven. He dismounted and studied the prints.

Evidently the rustlers were cautious—their drives from all directions had been small. Evidently they made many stealthy raids and no big ones.

He climbed atop a crag and looked around him.

At that moment Carter Slade, riding higher, saw him and fired those two quick wild shots.

Their sharp *zing* floated down to Kane. He leaped from the crag for the shelter of the brush.

The moment he fired, Carter Slade realized his mistake. He replaced his rifle in its scabbard and galloped across the rimtop for the shelter of the Crown.

Carter was confident that Kane hadn't seen him. Two shots from high above—how could a man know who had fired them?

But Kane's trained ears knew the direction the galloping horse was taking, that the rider was coming down the rim instead of going over it. He threw himself into the saddle and set out in hot pursuit. But the start Carter had was too much and Kane soon abandoned the chase, not, however, until he was sure that his assailant had cut across the rim road and onto Crown land, riding straight for Crown headquarters.

He found Carter's trail and followed it back to the rim, to the secret pass. Kane was not a detective—he never made deductions. He simply investigated all leads and let the results add up.

Some man from the Crown knew the secret of the high pass. Some man from the Crown regarded Ed Kane's approach to the pass as a threat to his security. Had he made a guess at the moment, he would have said Peck Purdy.

The first shadows were stealing down from the

rim when he reached the heights again. He picked off a cottontail with a quick shot and cooked it over a small sage fire in one of the recesses. Now, with the graying darkness, a chill came in the wind. His black mare settled against it as he resumed his climbing. No lights showed, except for the wash of stars glittering faintly above him. He turned boldly into the pass.

At times boldness was the most cautious policy.

The moon came up, yellow and overflowing, and he saw that cattle marks were plentiful here. The rimtop was no more than a mile wide, and already the country was breaking away on either side of him, falling into sharp shallows and steep jutting ridges. This trail wound in and out among them. It had been chosen with ingenuity, and it was not surprising that no valley man had ever suspected its presence.

Room to ride on either side of the trail now appeared, and he left the cattle path for the shelter alee. There was no question but what the trail he now paralleled was the main run, the chief highway over the rim. Beef was driven along this route to some destination ahead.

He pushed his way to a small knob overgrown with pine, left his horse and walked on until he could see the trail below by eerie shivering moonlight. It made its brown streaked way deviously along the footslopes of all the close-crowded ridges, crossing a creek that sent up a dull flash through the windy night's screen, and vanished again in the heavier shadows ahead. All around him the broken land reared shoulder after shoulder.

He remounted and rode slowly along this upper ridge. The terrain was changing now, was falling down from the spine of the rim to the flatter and less timbered lands they had always known as "the wastes." It was rock here and splintered shale and no cattle could graze. But beef could be driven through it, and in these yellow and brown upthrusts a man might hide forever. Cattle could follow this trail into the south plains, where they would be close to Mexico.

For an hour Ed Kane saw no sign. Then he glimpsed a light through the quivering pines, and knew a camp was nearby. It was a shack sitting off the trail, a quarter mile out in the plain. He rode until a dog's barking brought a shifting of the light and a scuffle of feet outside the cabin. Then he slipped from the saddle and went ahead on foot, moving noiselessly, slipping from shadow to shadow.

He went wide, slipping downwind from the dog. For a while all was jet dark under the timber and he had to depend on his instincts for directions. Then he saw a red eye gleaming farther ahead, and caught the smell of smoke and horses. He went forward a yard or so, crawling with the gentleness of a cat, his nerves as spooky and alert as a cat's.

The dog barked again, from behind the cabin, still investigating the sounds Ed Kane had made before he began his circling.

The door opened with a curse and a black-bearded man came outside with his rifle over his arm.

"What is it, Runt? If it's just a rabbit, I'll wear out a rope's end on you."

Kane slid along the edge of the cabin until he was directly behind this man, whose eyes were not yet used to the darkness.

"Hardly a rabbit, friend," he said gently. "Lift 'em up and turn around slow."

He was obeyed promptly.

"Now inside," Kane ordered.

He stepped in after his captive, pulling the door shut, kicking the rifle away.

Then he studied his man. A familiar type to Ed Kane, though he had never seen this particular one before. But there had been dozens of others just like him, heavy-bearded and sharp-eyed, scar-faced, stoop-shouldered, sharp-mouthed. Some Rangers would arrest such a man on sight.

"My name's Kane," he said softly.

He was not altogether without his pride. He realized what the name Kane meant to such men. Riders of the Whisper Trail knew every Ranger and every sheriff. From these men, who had good cause to know, one could get an unbiased evaluation of what a lawman was.

An answering gleam shone in this bearded man's eyes. It was followed by a thin, mirthless smile.

"Kane, huh?"

He shrugged his shoulders and sat down on a wide low bunk. Kane reached over and jerked back the covers. No gun was concealed among them.

"You quit the Rangers, didn't you?" he was asked.

"Yes. I came trailing my own cattle. Where will I find 'em?"

"Don't rush me," was the grinning answer. "What's the deal?"

"No deal," Kane snapped.

"Don't be a fool. Take me in and what do you have? A whipping boy. This ain't a one-man outfit, Kane. You know that."

"I know that," Ed admitted.

He thought, as he studied the man's dark, grinning face, that outlaws, more than honest men, showed keen senses of humor. This bearded man, though trying to bargain for his life, was unafraid. He had met his match—it did not worry him. Kane could understand that. Lawmen riding after them, on the same dangerous trails, soon feel that way themselves—that sooner or later they must inevitably meet their match.

"I don't want my neck stretched," yawned the black-visaged man. "If you were smart enough to trail me over the rim, and get by my dog, you know the layout."

"I know it," Kane nodded.

He said no more. Let the prisoner talk.

"But you can't follow the tracks of the man—the men—who figgered this out. They don't mean nothin' to me, Kane. They ain't dealt too well with me in the first place. What's it worth to talk—and straight?"

"What do you want?"

"A running start with a fresh horse."

"I can't give you that."

A shrug. "You're prodding the spread."

"Other men have lost cattle."

Another shrug.

"Who are you?"

"Black Ben's enough."

"I guess. Where do these cattle go?"

"Friend," yawned Black Ben, "I can't hear a word you're saying. Unless you want to start riding now, I'm turning in. Need my beauty sleep."

"You sure do," smiled Kane. "About twenty years of it."

"Good Rangers," Ben grinned back, "never bully their prisoners."

"I'm not a Ranger anymore."

"You still got the marks."

Kane hesitated. He could carry this man back over the rim and into Cotulla. But evidence might prove skimpy. And he was willing to concede Black Ben couldn't be made to talk. Men like Black Ben were sometimes pretty stubborn.

"Kinda got you over the barrel, ain't I?" grinned the outlaw. "You gotta play my way, Kane. A fresh horse and a running start."

"How can I promise that?" Ed parried. "I'm not the law. I'm just one man who lost cattle. The others might look at it differently."

Another shrug.

Kane deliberated. As he had said, Black Ben was unimportant. Another man could do this as well. Taking Black Ben in would settle nothing. Besides, he had a sudden distaste against arresting another man. That was no longer his job.

"All right, Ben," he nodded. "I'll deal. You hang out here a couple of days. I'll go back into the valley and talk to my friends. Then we'll come after you—and you can talk to the man you accuse face to face."

Ben's face fell. "That ain't my proposition. How will I know about the running start?"

"That's the best I can do. Take it or leave it."

"I don't wanna go back over there, Kane. You know ranch folks sometimes get excited."

"I'll keep them under control."

"And I don't want no truck with a sheriff. I wanna—"

"We aren't calling in the sheriff," Kane interrupted. "One of our valley men is ramrodding this. We can keep the law in our own valley."

"Two or three days!" mused Black Ben. "How

do you know I'll still be here? What's to keep me from . . ."

"I got ideas about that," Kane smiled. He caught Ben as the outlaw lay loose on the bunk.

"Hey! What's this?" demanded Black Ben. But he did not resist.

Kane took a rawhide riato from the wall. "Nice of you to keep things like this around, Black Ben. I plumb appreciate it."

"You can't leave me tied up here two or three days!" wailed the rustler. "That ain't human, Kane. No good Ranger . . .

"I'm not a Ranger," snapped Ed.

He finished his job. "Sabbe those knots, Ben?" he asked. "They're loose. But if you try to get away, they'll pull tight. If you jerk on 'em, God help you. They'll cut your wrists and legs right in two."

"Kane, dammit, I can't . . ."

"I'm fixing you food and water," Ed broke in. "You'll get by. I don't call it living in comfort, but you'll get by. I want you here when I ride back this way."

He cooked bacon and beans under Black Ben's angry eyes. He set water by the bunk, a pail of it and a tin cup. Ben could move enough to feed himself, and to fill the cup.

"Now," Kane grinned, "you can catch up on your beauty sleep."

"Look, Kane, fan the breeze, will you?" Ben

appealed. “This ain’t no way to treat a man. I tell you I’ll talk. I’ll . . .”

“I followed a trail back to the Crown, Ben,” Ed explained. “I got my hunches.”

“But it’s the other guy who started it. Don’t go off half-cocked.”

“You can tell your story to the boys. I’ll round ’em up and we’ll listen to you.”

“And I get my running start?”

“You get all you want,” Kane shrugged.

7

TOMMY MCGEE rode into Cotulla and stopped for a drink at the bar. His brother eyed him nervously.

“I gotta charge you for it,” Jerry reminded him. Tommy seemed to feel that because his brother was a bartender, he didn’t have to pay for his drinks. Fats Haley, the saloon owner, had a different idea. In fact, Fats had threatened to fire Jerry if he was caught again doling out free liquor to his relatives.

In answer Tommy laid down a gold piece. “Make it a double,” he ordered.

Jerry was surprised. “Where did you get it?” he demanded suspiciously.

“None of your worry,” Tommy barked. “You just wait on a cash customer like you’re paid to.”

Tommy had other gold pieces. There was a

bounty on wolves and coyotes. Some winters Tommy trapped many of them. He had no less than a hundred dollars in gold carefully wrapped in his jeans pockets. No telling how many years Tommy had saved his money. He had not spent it, because a McGee was not expected to pay for what he ate or bought, except articles like shells, tobacco and jeans. He had not spent it, because what money bought had never tempted a McGee, who knew little about such things.

But now Tommy downed his whisky and went into the hotel and registered for a room. Again he was required to pay in advance.

He went upstairs and washed. He was more presentable than any other McGee ever looked, as he came downstairs into the dining room for supper. His sister, back from her rendezvous with Davis Conroy, gaped at him.

"Why, Tommy!"

"Bring me the steak," he ordered gruffly.

He leaned back and rolled a smoke. Jeremiah was eating across the room. It was said Jeremiah ate a cold dinner in his office and this supper at the hotel was the only decent meal he had a day. Tommy grinned. Suddenly he felt a little superior to Jeremiah. And to Mary, his sister.

She brought him his coffee and he took it with a nod. Mary studied his face, then walked to another table, shaking her head. What had come over Tommy? In the saloon Jerry was explaining to Fats

Haley that his brother had paid for his drink in gold.

"Walked in here putting on airs as if he was somebody," Jerry said in disgust. "Reckon he robbed a bank?"

Fats laughed derisively. "Reckon not," Jerry admitted. "He wouldn't have the nerve."

There wasn't much family loyalty among the McGees.

Tommy ate his supper slowly. He had always wanted to eat here, but never had done so until he was held for trial and the county paid for his grub. Eating here made him feel important.

He rolled another cigarette, when he had finished, and leaned back in his chair, loath to leave this comfortable place. Mary tried to chat with him as she cleaned off his table but he wasn't in a mood for conversation. He watched his sister through narrowed eyelids. Her and Davis Conroy! What would she say if she knew that he had come to town to wait for Davis Conroy! And meant to kill him.

He hung around the saloon until ten o'clock, then went to bed. In the morning he had a "snort before breakfast," another long cherished ambition. Then eggs over. And an extra cup of coffee.

"Tommy, where did you get the money for this?" demanded Mary.

He disdained to answer. It was strange that, while he intended to kill the man who had seduced his sister, he was not actually interested in that sister. He did not regard any of his brothers or his parents with affection. They were McGees like him, and thus not worth much.

He did not stop to reason that he was gunning for Davis Conroy not because of Mary but because of Carter Slade and Calhoun Conroy. Tommy's philosophical thought did not go that far.

On the afternoon of the second day Davis Conroy rode into town with Carter Slade, Peck Purdy and two other Crown hands. It was Saturday afternoon and Tommy's face lit up as he saw the crowd in the saloon, where Davis and Slade had gone while the other Crown men took their horses to the livery stable. He was glad there would be people around. He wanted everybody to see this—a McGee standing up to a Conroy.

He sauntered into the saloon, trying to act nonchalant and move lazily as he had seen Ed Kane move. His gun was oiled until it shone and rubbed grease on his jeans.

Conroy was drinking with Slade at the bar, their backs to McGee.

"You ain't particular who you drink with, are you, Slade?" Tommy drawled.

There wasn't a sound for a long minute. Tommy had waited for a lull in the whirlpools of conversation before making his taunt. Every man in the saloon heard him. There were the Winslows and the

Cumberlands and several riders from the Short T spread below the rim.

Both Carter and Davis whirled. Tommy stood rocking on his heels, one hand close to his holster, a sneer on his scrawny face.

"Yeah, I mean you, Conroy," he snapped. "Carter ain't much to associate with himself but you're the lowest down maverick in these parts. You ain't much better than a stinking sheep."

"What the hell is this?" demanded Slade. "Get out of here, McGee, before I kick your teeth in."

"Stay out of this, Slade," ordered Tommy. "I'm talking to Conroy."

Every eye in the saloon was trained expectantly upon Davis Conroy. No man in this country had ever been so publicly insulted without doing something about it. They were shocked that Tommy McGee had done it. They were more surprised when Conroy's face turned a deep red, his hands trembled, and he turned back to the bar.

"Gimme another drink," he said hoarsely to Jerry.

Jerry was standing as if petrified, unable to believe what he had heard and seen. His brother hurling a challenge in a Conroy's face here in a public saloon!

Carter was also amazed. He was no gunman himself, and had refused to draw against McGee in the dusty street after the trial. But he would not have tolerated this kind of talk from anyone.

Yet Carter was enjoying it. He hated all the Conroys, Davis more than any. Peck Purdy strolled in and saw there was trouble. He edged forward, quick to show his strange kind of loyalty. Carter waved him back.

"Just a private fuss," said Slade. "McGee here has it in for Davis."

Davis flashed an appealing look around him. He wanted to cry out to these men his explanation of his refusal to draw upon Tommy McGee, especially when the slight, scrawny-faced man came forward another step and drawled:

"Make your play whenever you want it, Davis."

Davis licked his lips. Carter watched with a cold smile. It occurred to Carter that it would be much easier for him if Davis was to draw and Tommy McGee was to surprise them with a swift sure shot that would leave the youngest Conroy dead on the saloon floor. But that was too much to hope for. Or was it? Carter had a sneaking respect for McGee's marksmanship. The Crown had paid bounty money to Tommy for killing wolves. Perhaps, now that the little bastard had worked up his nerve, he could put up a fight.

But Davis did not intend to draw. That was obvious. No man present could understand it, not even the Cumberlands and the Winslows, who were glorying in this public humiliation of a Conroy.

"Damn you, McGee," whispered Davis. "You know—I can't pull on you."

Tommy laughed. It was a wild sort of laugh. After a man has spent his lifetime cowering before other men, it does something to him to have the situation reversed, to have a man tremble before him, especially when that man is the son of Calhoun Conroy.

He reached out and slapped Davis' face. A stinging slap with his wide-open palm.

"Get out, Conroy," he growled. Davis towered over him by half a head and weighed at least fifty pounds more. "Get outside. Don't take up space in the saloon that is meant for men."

Davis was trembling. It was next to impossible to hold back the urge to shake this little scrawny man and then to kill him, and, perhaps, to stomp on his lifeless body. But a man cannot shoot down the brother of the girl he intends to marry.

"We'll get out," he conceded. "Come on, Slade."

Carter laughed. "Not me, Davis. I'm not running from the little whelp. Tuck your tail between your legs and get out if you want to."

Carter hoped to goad the youngest Conroy into a fight. Anyhow, he wanted to rub in the humiliation. Like Tommy McGee, he was enjoying the spectacle of a Conroy wilting. Though the Conroys trusted him and paid him well, they had always made it plain that he was a hired man and thus beneath them.

Davis staggered out. Mocking laughter followed

him. The Cumberlands laughed. And Carter loudest of all.

The only man who didn't snicker was Peck Purdy. The tall gunman watched his foreman with a queer expression in his narrow gray eyes. Those same eyes finally came to McGee's face. Carter thought of Peck Purdy as a witless man who rode an outlaw trail and who could shoot with the cunning and speed of a wild thing. He had never inquired about Purdy's antecedents. He would have been shocked to have learned that once this gun-slick had attended college, and that even now, when the opportunity presented itself, Purdy read good books and thought intelligent thoughts.

Purdy had his job, and he would do it. But he would wonder about that job, and about the man who hired him.

Tommy's face was flushed with triumph. He had meant to kill Davis Conroy, but he was glad that hadn't been necessary. He had shown those men that a McGee could stand up and bark his challenge. He had worn a chip on his shoulder as he had always dreamed of doing, and that chip was still there—the son of Calhoun Conroy had been afraid to knock it off. Tommy, of course, could not attribute Davis' hesitancy to any other motive than actual fear.

He turned to Carter Slade. This man he did not like either. He recalled that he had offered to fight this man, and that Carter had also refused. Nor did he stop to recall that Carter had turned away because Ed Kane had stepped out of the courtyard to stand at a McGee's side.

"You Crown men ain't so tough," Tommy sneered.

In this mood he was not even afraid of Peck Purdy. He became the first man to speak up to the Crown with Purdy around. Even the Winslows, tough grim fighters, didn't do that. The valley knew that Purdy was a gun-slick from Arizona and they were careful not to give him an excuse for dragging his guns out and blazing away. They knew why Carter Slade had hired him.

"Look, Shorty," growled Carter. "Just because one man ran from you, don't get any notions you're the cock of the walk. You're still a cheap rustler in my books."

"And you're still a blow-hard in mine," Tommy shot back.

He turned on his heel and swaggered out of the saloon. Carter downed his drink and followed him.

Outside, with Purdy a dozen steps behind, Slade called to McGee.

"Mebbe you wanna carry on the conversation we started inside?" Carter asked with narrow eyes. "Mebbe you want to add some more to your opinion of me?"

"Reckon I said about all I need to," Tommy sneered. "I might add that I know a little more about you than you think I do, Slade. You see, I ride high on the rim myself."

He was hinting at Slade's visit to Jeremiah Gilbert. But the frowning, suddenly panicky Carter Slade thought he meant something else—the concealed pass through the rimtops, the beaten cattle trail over which a thousand head of valley cattle had been driven in the past year.

Carter Slade might have drawn on him had he not made that sly reference to "riding high on the rim." Now Carter wouldn't. This scrawny little man was dangerous. The anger Carter had felt in the saloon disappeared. He was his normal cold, calculating self again. He whirled on his heel and stamped away, motioning for Purdy to follow.

"Get that man and don't be long about it," he snapped. "He's feeling his oats. Probably he'll cut loose his wolf tonight. If you bait him, he'll give you a chance."

"Don't want to do your own killing?" Purdy asked softly.

"I can't afford to take a chance," Carter snapped. "Besides, that's what I hired you for, ain't it?"

"Sometimes I wonder *what* you hired me for," Peck said slowly. "If the button gives me trouble, I'll take him on. I ain't shooting him down in cold blood, Slade."

Carter studied this tall thin man a moment with angry eyes. He felt himself superior to Purdy's type of roving, penniless gunman.

"See that you 'tend to him," he ordered.

He went to the livery stable. Davis was already in his saddle and riding away. The youngest Conroy did not even speak to the Crown foreman. Carter smiled unpleasantly.

Purdy returned to the saloon. Now McGee was drinking again, flushed with his two triumphs. The two men he hated most in the valley had backed away from him. He was regretting the years he had spent in mute acceptance of his family's inferiority. He patted his gun and addressed the Winslows and Cumberlands.

"The McGees have been kicked around in this valley long enough," he declaimed. "From now on, people who don't wanna treat us as equals can stay out of our trail."

Purdy slid against the bar. Jerry set him out a drink.

Tommy turned scornful eyes upon the gun-slick.

"I thought I run all of you Crown men outa town!"

"Easy," Purdy said softly.

Purdy had meant every word of what he had told Carter. He would not shoot Tommy McGee in cold blood. He would not even deliberately seek out a fight with the inflamed little man. But that, he knew, was only a slight concession to his conscience. He had known that when he walked back into this saloon Tommy McGee would notice him and give him the opening he must have. He told himself, even as he grinned coldly at McGee, that he was doing just what Slade had ordered him to do, that he was plotting cold-blooded murder and doing no more than set up the circumstances that would free him from arrest, or another flight.

"Looks like working for that outfit would turn a man's stomach," Tommy croaked. "It would—a white man's."

Here was Purdy's chance.

"What would you be knowing about white men?" he demanded. "They tell me that a McGee is nothing more than a cross-breed between a Spick and a coyote."

The liquor, as well as the sudden feeling of importance, had gone to Tommy McGee's head. He was actually looking down from his imaginary height upon this tall slim man. No man could talk to him like that—and live.

He cursed and grabbed at his gun. It was halfway out of his holster before Purdy moved. Even at this moment Purdy had to salve that queer conscience of his, what was left of it.

McGee shot too quickly. He had to, for he saw, as he lifted his eyes, that Purdy was moving with the incredible swiftness of his kind. Be it said to Tommy's credit that in this split second he realized the inevitability of his fate, and did his best calmly. He took a calculated chance, an instinctive chance, with a quick shot. Never even raised his gun for it.

His bullet tore through Purdy's sleeve, singeing the tall man's flesh.

Then there was another roar and Tommy McGee dropped his gun and slipped to the floor.

A surprised look came in his eyes, as if it were incredible that this could be happening to him. He clawed at the empty air for support. It wasn't there. He slumped to the floor and rolled forward on his face.

Purdy replaced the smoking gun in his holster. His gray eyes studied the men around him—Jeff Winslow and Matthew Cumberland had left their place at the bar and stepped forward.

"Reckon he asked for it," Purdy said coldly.

No man there could deny that. Tommy McGee had cut loose his wolf and had been shot down in self-defense. He had kept looking for a fight until he had found it.

"The danged fool got what was coming to him," Jerry McGee said harshly from behind the bar.

8

MARY WAS LEFT alone with her brother's small stiff body. She had cried at first. Now she looked down upon what had been Tommy McGee with mingled emotions, among which was one of envy. At least he was at peace. At least he was free from the stranglehold thrown around every McGee at birth, and from which there seemed no escape.

It was late. The sheriff had asked questions and then, with a shrug of his shoulders, had ordered Tommy's body carried to his office to await burial. Despite Jerry's protests that he was tired after working all day, he had been dispatched to inform Sam McGee.

She looked down upon Tommy and wondered why she could summon only an impersonal grief. She had cried, yes. She wanted to cry again. He was so small and his existence had been so warped. He had fought back where no other McGee had ever dared, not once but twice. He had fought with a courage and a skill no one had thought a McGee could own. The usual valley cruelty had been unable to suppress him—he had grinned in its teeth and gone swaggering on his queer, lonely way. But this valley hired outside strength when its own failed. Mary could remember other Peck Purdys. A long time ago, when she had been only a girl, the Crown had brought in not one but a half dozen. That was when the Conroys were pushing up from their original spread on Cypress Creek.

Some men had fought back and had been killed. She couldn't remember just who.

But they had been killed fighting for something tangible. What had Tommy McGee been fighting for? She had no way of knowing, of course, that he had looked down from the rimtop upon her assignation with Davis. She would not have believed this had inspired Tommy's sudden defiance if she had known it. And that alone *had* not. It had taken many things. Tommy had found a refuge where the other McGees had not—the high rim where valley men did not ride. There he had nursed his small resentments until they became a creed. Then Ed Kane returned and, in a single awful moment, when the Crown guns hung loose and free, he had found an ally. His sister never had. Nor the other McGees.

With a start she realized the lateness of the hour and that soon Sam McGee and her mother would come into Cotulla to take the body. She had no wish to see them. Sam had driven her away from the small nester's cabin when the first slur fell upon her reputation. It was queer that Sam, who had no other pride, could not tolerate immorality, at least of this type. He had never tried to stop Jerry and Tommy from stealing off into the darkness and returning with a butchered yearling, though the McGees had never owned any livestock other than a milch cow. But a daughter who was loose with men—he could not tolerate this. She must go and never darken his door again. A woman has only one way of being loose, and that is unpardonable. A man has several, and all of them can be explained unto appeasement.

She pulled the tablecloth—in lieu of a sheet—over Tommy's face and left the courthouse. Her horse was outside. With her first money from the restaurant she had bought herself a horse and a saddle. It was a good mount, as good as any the Conroys rode. The town sneered that she had earned this "paint"—the valley's name for her type of horse—with her outside activities, but that was only base slander. Never had Mary given herself to a man for money. She was the last person to attempt an explanation if someone ever had asked, "Then why did you?"

At first she had no destination. Then, after several minutes in the clear, open night, she decided to ride to Kane's. Perhaps she was clutching at a straw in deciding that, since Tommy had worked for Ed, it was her duty to notify Kane. Had she stopped to deliberate she would have realized that precious little work had Tommy ever done for anyone, and that her brother's failure to appear at Ed's corral in the morning would not upset Kane's routine in the least.

But Mary never stopped to analyze why she did things, or to argue herself out of doing them. She wanted to see Kane. She wanted to tell him about Tommy's death. She spurred her horse into a gallop. With Mary, action was almost simultaneous with thought.

The hour was past two when she reached the small frame cottage perched precariously on the back side of the benchland, an easy target for any avalanche of boulders from the rim above. Kane heard the sound of her horse even before she called out, and was at the front window watching silently when she came on the porch and called "Ed."

"Just a moment, Mary."

As he dressed, he searched his own thoughts. It was natural, perhaps, that he credit her with a different motive than her desire to tell him about Tommy's death. No man could help that. And yet, even yet, he had a wholesome respect for Mary as a person. He had been unhappy to learn that she and Davis Conroy were using his family's deserted house as a meeting spot, but he had been thinking since that day he had called Davis on the trail, and the younger Conroy had so heatedly answered. Nothing of the slinking dog about Davis that day. A man cannot pretend a feeling like that.

He opened the door and she went right into his arms with a suddenness that left him gasping. She clung to him when he tried to push her back, and there on his shoulder she turned loose the tears she had been able to control in the sheriff's office.

"What in the world, child?" he demanded.

Even as he was conscious of her as a woman, and was tingling from the nearness of her hair and her well-developed body, he called her "child," and did so kindly. It is possible that a man can feel two things at once.

"Ed—Tommy was killed."

He stiffened. There was no reason for him to take Tommy's battles as his own. But he had once, acting impulsively and without thought, and it was like Ed Kane that one such action committed him to a loyalty.

"Slade?" he demanded.

There was a hangover of his loyalty to Carter—Ed Kane's feelings did not die easily. But if the two loyalties clashed as they had once—!

"No, Peck Purdy."

"Damn him," grated Kane. Now he did push her off. Purdy! He liked the man. He even had a sympathy for the man's type. But the years with the Rangers, when he and this type of man were sworn enemies, had left their impression.

"He couldn't help it, Ed. Tommy forced it on him."

She described what she had heard second-hand, that Tommy had called out Davis Conroy, and Davis had run. Then her brother had hurled his challenge at Slade, and the foreman had shrugged it off. Purdy did not step back. Kane's anger cooled. He knew how to look at such a thing from the gunman's viewpoint. There had been that cocky, grinning youngster calling Purdy, swaggering right into the barrel of his gun. A gunman couldn't run just because he was that—a gunman.

"I see," he murmured.

Without asking, he set the iron coffeepot on the stove and kindled a fire. As at other ranches, his coffeepot was always full, ready to be warmed and served.

He helped Mary to a chair and she sat quivering,

her gaze on the floor. He rolled a cigarette with slow, uncertain fingers.

"I hate that, Mary," he faltered. It was hard to know what he should say. "I had begun to believe there was hope for Tommy."

"And there isn't for any other McGee," she snapped, raising her head. "Say it, Ed. We're all rotten. Tommy was the best of a bad lot. He had the nerve to try and act like a man. And he was shot down."

Her voice softened and she avoided his gaze. "Perhaps Tommy," she murmured, "isn't the first McGee—to be shot down."

"I didn't mean that," he said hurriedly. "I didn't mean anything like that. I meant I had just come to know Tommy. I think he was honest. I think he was capable of loyalty. He didn't make me a good hand but he couldn't help that. He didn't like work like mine—humdrum, detail work. I'm sorry, Mary, that's all."

Her black head went down again. "I shouldn't have flared up," she apologized. "No call to bark at you like that."

The coffee was ready. He poured her a cup. He watched her in silence as she downed it in two gulps, and held out her cup for more. He sipped his slowly. Now she seemed to have conquered her grief. Now her voice was a little brittle, and a little bitter.

"I don't know why one McGee more or less

makes any difference," she shrugged. "I think if it had been Jerry, I would have been glad—honestly glad."

She gave him a direct, level gaze. "Jerry was always trying to get me out," she explained. "Me, his own sister."

Ed's lips tightened. How could he respond to that? Sympathy? Anger?

"I think I've stood it as long as I can," she mused. "I don't know why I haven't left before. There isn't much for me anywhere else—just, I guess, the life I've led here. But I think I would be happier."

He knew she meant Davis. He nodded.

"Life does get a little messed up sometimes," he sighed. Now he was thinking about Catherine Conroy. Already regret had begun to set in. He could not be sure that Catherine was the answer to the personal enigma that had haunted him of late, but he regretted that he had driven her off before such a thing could be learned for sure. Lingering doubt eventually overcomes all arguments.

"You have nothing to be unhappy about," Mary said. "You are a man. What is bothering you can be changed. You can leave and find another range. A woman can do only one thing, Ed. She can find a man. And, with a woman, it has to be her first man."

"I wouldn't say that," he comforted. It was an

idle speech—even while he made it he knew she was right. "There is always a second chance. And a third."

He hesitated. "What's the matter with Davis?" he finally asked.

"Davis is—Davis."

She left him wondering what she meant, for she didn't mention the name again.

She laid her head on the pine kitchen table and burst into tears. He watched her in silence. Not many forms of human emotion had evaded Ed Kane's restless eyes, but this was one he had never learned how to handle. Besides, how could you soothe a crying woman when you didn't know what she was crying about?

He was not narrow-minded enough just to dismiss this as a mood. He knew that it wasn't. For a long time Mary McGee had had this coming on, since before Ed Kane had ridden away. Ed remembered such a feeling himself. A man could drink his into surrender. For a woman there was not even the comfort of drink. He could offer her sympathy. But how?

For a long time afterward Ed Kane wondered what had ever come over him to make him think of such a thing. He crushed out his cigarette and reached for her with his long arms, picked her up clear of the straight-back chair and the pine table, and carried her onto the front porch, where he sat of evenings and rocked and smoked and planned what he would do the next day, and days long after. He sat down with her in the rocking chair and began to rock gently back and forth. He thought she would never stop crying. Even after she was hoarse, her voice almost gone, her crying became small breathless gasps, her body still shaking with it.

Eventually the nearness of her, and the fragrance of her hair, caused Ed to think of her with another feeling. Her crying stopped and she raised her head and smiled at him.

Without thinking he kissed her and tightened the grip of his arm. No man could have done otherwise.

She lay motionless. She did not resist. Her eyes were closed and her body was lax in mute surrender.

He raised his head and stared at her, a gleam in his eyes that Mary McGee knew full well.

She opened her eyes and studied his face with a peaceful gaze.

"No, Ed," she said gently. "At least—not tonight."

He nodded. Satisfied with her answer, and his acceptance, he brought her head back against his shoulder and rocked again. Within a moment she was asleep, sound asleep. She did not even open her eyes as he picked her up and carried her inside, to lay her on his bed and cover her with a blanket. Ed looked down at her.

"I'll be damned," he muttered.

He slept on the floor for the short time that remained until daylight. But it was a restless sleep from which he awoke many times. He was glad when morning came.

He had bacon sputtering in the pan and fresh coffee boiling when Mary awoke. She gave him a light good morning, and he smiled at her casualness as she washed her face and sat at the table with an air of mild impatience. She ate heartily, lingering over her coffee. She did not seem inclined to talk and he did not press conversation upon her.

Actually that was Ed Kane's humor too. He was thinking hard. She finished breakfast and offered to do the dishes. He declined. Mary studied him a moment and then rode off with a "So long, Ed." She gave him no thanks for his understanding treatment of her in the early morning hours. Perhaps, knowing him better than he would ever imagine, she realized such an expression of gratitude was not necessary, and that he, as well as herself, would appreciate it if the details of that night were never brought up.

She felt a strange lightness as she loped her paint back toward Cotulla. Dejection was out of her system. She had cried out her bitterness and her unhappiness. Now she was, for the moment, completely reconciled. She had referred to an escape—she knew there was none. But not since she was a little girl had Mary McGee been so nearly happy with her lot.

It was as if she had left all her restlessness and dissatisfaction and worry in Ed Kane's house, as if it had been tossed from her shoulders onto his.

As for Ed, he frowned at his coffee. He carried a fresh cup onto the porch and sat in the rocking chair and continued to frown.

Life in the shadow of the rim was no cinch for a man either. Ed Kane had no commitments and no heavy burdens of a past or a future. But the consciousness of the emptiness of his existence was weighing heavier and heavier upon him. It had driven him out of the Rangers and back to this valley and his father's benchland.

He had lost years that could never he recovered. All men did. He could reassure himself that these years weren't important, but he was poignantly aware of this fallacy. All years were important and the years that were just behind him most important of all.

Ed Kane did not have the patience of Carter Slade. Few things worried him for he was a man who did not believe in worry. But that type of man, when worry comes, is most affected by it, for it is strange to him, an emotion he does not understand. He is irritated by it and must find the solution at once, as if he could be master of his life and must mold it to his immediate demands.

Ed Kane's only answer to worry was action. He

left his soiled cup on the porch and stamped to the corral. His horse whinnied resentment—here the sun was high, almost nine o'clock, and it had not yet been fed and watered. Perhaps, if Kane could have understood horse talk, he would have had the long dangerous trails of his past thrown up to him. As it was, he patted the horse, threw in an extra shovelful of oats and all was well. A man is born knowing how to handle horses.

Eventually, without returning to the house, he rode straight across the benchland toward the timber he had purchased from Jeremiah Gilbert, and to a clearing that was no more than a bald spot on the shaggy, rough bear's hide that was the side of Sunset Rim.

He heard the sound of an ax as he rode nearer. In his queer aimless fashion Sam McGee was an industrious man. He sold cedar posts to the ranchmen, sometimes firewood as well, and he threw up flood gaps for most of the valley spreads. Kane called to him and the ringing stopped. Sam shouted out from a near-by cedar patch:

"Who is it?"

"Ed Kane."

Ed dismounted. McGee came out of the cedars. He was small, as were all the McGee men. His heard was a coarse tangle around his pinched, narrow features and his eyes were as furtive as Tommy's. Had Tommy lived another forty years he might have become the spit'n image of his father.

The cabin was a stone's throw away, a two-room, unsteady affair with a cedar roof. Though skillful with an ax, even to making comfortable chairs and tables for the near-by ranches, Samuel McGee had never bothered much about his own shack. Any roof, it seemed, would do. He had moved from one deserted line cabin to another, sometimes on the Winslow land, sometimes in Jeremiah Gilbert's timber. Only Jeremiah and the Crown resented the presence of Sam and his family.

Now, at the sound of voices, the family poured out of the two-room house and stood gawking in wonder. After a moment, Sam's wife returned to her washing. In her life there was no time for visiting.

There were four kids, one still in diapers, although at least two years beyond the stage. Nobody had even been sure just how many McGees there were.

"Kane, huh?"

Sam did not offer to shake hands. The gesture would have left him blinking if Kane had made it. A nester's presence might be tolerated, but no one shook hands with him.

It occurred to Ed that this was the first time in his life he had ever talked face to face with Sam McGee, though once the nester pack had lived in his father's back pasture, and Mrs. McGee had come to the back door more than once to beg a loan from his mother—lard or flavoring or torn soiled sheets which would make diapers for the babies.

"I'm sorry about Tommy," Ed said. "When is the funeral?"

"Held this morning," was the terse unsentimental explanation. "In the Sadler burying ground. Larry made the offer."

Ed nodded. That was like Larry Sadler, who kept the post office and general store. A soft-hearted sort of man who lost what profits he could have made by extending credit too freely. It was said the Crown still owed him money for a drought credit. Sadler never pushed anybody for payment.

"I wish I could have been there," Ed said. Mary must have missed the funeral also.

"The Lord gives them and the Lord takes them away," Sam said. "I won't say I'm grieving much, Mister Kane. My kids have been a trial, as you know. None of 'em would take their father's teachings."

Inside Ed Kane a voice sneered "hypocrite." What had been Sam McGee's teachings? To be worthless and aimless, to be meek and servile, to be content with slovenliness and filth and want. No wonder each McGee, as soon as he was big enough to toddle away, sought a different answer than the one ready-made for him.

"Still death is sad," Ed said. "I liked Tommy. He had a job with me as long as he wanted it."

"It was good of you to take him in," Sam McGee sighed. "I heard about it and thought maybe at last one of my brood was headed in the right direction. But likker got in him, and likker is no good for any man, Mister Kane. Tommy got out of his place. His punishment was stern, but I figger it was just. I got no kick against this man Purdy."

Ed sat down on a cedar stump and pulled out his sack of tobacco. Sam McGee refused—he was chewing on thick-cut.

"I really came to talk about Mary," he said awkwardly. This was something new to him. To talk sentimentally about a woman is always new and strange and hard for any man.

"We don't talk about Mary," Sam rasped. "She made her bed and she can lie on it."

Ed's lips quirked.

"I want to marry her," he said calmly.

"Marry her!"

Sam McGee's voice was hoarse with astonishment.

"Yes," Ed said calmly.

"Mister Kane, I don't—Mary is—well, hang it, man, you don't want my gal! Mebbe you've been gone from this valley so long you don't know. I reckon it's my Christian duty to tell you . . ."

"Isn't that my affair—and hers?" Ed broke in softly.

"I guess so," McGee sighed.

He sat down on another near-by stump. He sat

down weakly, as if standing any longer was a physical impossibility.

"That shore beats a hawg a-flying," he whispered. "I don't know what to say, Mister Kane. I ain't got my wits around me anymore."

"Is there anything to say?" Ed demanded. "You know, of course, that I wouldn't let your opposition stop me anyhow."

Again Sam McGee gasped. Here was Ed Kane, the son of Henry Kane, a man who owned land and cattle and a decent house, who could walk into the front door of any home in the valley, asking humbly for permission to marry his daughter, a McGee.

"What are you asking me fer!" he demanded. "None of you ever asked me if you could court Mary, or carry her out into the bushes. Nobody ever paid any attention to her father before."

"I want to get married," Ed said slowly. "Mary is the woman I want to marry. I'm asking you, as a man ought to ask any woman's father."

"Do you mean that, Mister Kane?" demanded McGee. "You ain't just wolfing an old man, are you? You wanna take my girl and get married before a preacher and take her to live with you?"

"That's right."

"In spite of her—what's she been? In spite of her brothers, including the one that's lying in the fresh dirt back in town? In spite of where she lived and what her pappy is?"

"That's right."

A tear shone in Sam McGee's faded eyes. "I ain't had a man treat me so in twenty year, Mister Kane," he mumbled. "It just—well, it takes the breath out of me. Me and the old woman there, we've been kicked around like dogs so long that I guess we are dogs. I beg your pardon, Mister Kane, for the way I've acted this day. I should have known you were like your pappy—no finer man ever lived than Henry Kane, and I don't mind telling you I cried like a woman the day they buried him there by the spring."

"Thank you," Ed murmured.

Sam leaped to his feet. "I feel myself just outright honored, Mister Kane. If my gal can marry you, I'll figger she's made up for all she's done, that somehow she has gotten forgiveness from Heaven for her life of sin. I want to shake your hand, Mister Kane, and to tell you that you've made Sam McGee feel like a different man this day. If I've raised a gal who can marry a man like you, I ain't done so bad after all. Now will you excuse me, Mister Kane? Please, sir, just ride on off."

"Why?" Kane asked wonderingly.

"Wal, sir," McGee answered, shifting his weight from foot to foot in embarrassment, "I want to pray a little, right here before I get the words off my mind. Many times in these twenty year I've figgered the good Lord musta forgot about Sam

McGee and his kind. But now I know it was just His way of testing our patience."

Ed Kane rode off with a queer feeling inside him. He had taken this step blindly, knowingly and defiantly rash in deciding to do so. But as he loped away from the clearing, he wondered if he had not done well—if perhaps Sam McGee's queer narrow faith might not be right, and if sometimes the people in the shadow of Sunset Rim did things through no fault or power of their own.

MARY MCGEE greeted Kane with a wan smile. "Coffee," he ordered, "and some of those sinkers there. Two or three."

She brought the coffee and doughnuts, then went away to wait on another customer. She returned to look down at him with a stirring gaze.

"You're the only man I ever had to thank for decent treatment, Ed," she said quietly. "It meant a lot to me. I think I can carry on now."

He stirred his coffee, avoiding her eyes. "I saw your father this morning," he said after a moment.

"Pappy?"

She asked no further explanation. It was obvious that he intended to say more.

"I had something to ask him," Kane murmured. "Maybe I should have asked you first."

She pretended to be busily wiping the counter before him with her damp cloth.

"I want to marry you, Mary," he told her finally.

The cloth stopped. But she did not raise her head. "Why?" she asked faintly in a small voice, a tiny voice coming from deep inside her.

"I thought you would ask that," he smiled. "I thought you would give me argument. All women do."

There was no answer. "I'm lonely, Mary. I need a wife. Once, when I was young, I thought I needed a princess. I thought I needed a woman who could be set up on a pedestal and gawked at by all the men around. I thought I wanted something fragile and unattainable. That was a boy's dream, Mary. Probably you know what I mean."

"Yes, I know," she agreed, a quirk to her full red lips.

"Now I'm older," he went on. "Now I've ridden some. I went riding looking—for a woman, as well as a lot of other things. There was one hill and then there was another. All of 'em, after a while, got to looking about the same. Then I stopped riding and took stock of what I had. Just what I rode away with, Mary. Me. And a horse."

The counter needed her attention again. He raised his coffee to his lips as he paused and it seemed to her that he had made a little splash on the shining surface. Or did she imagine it?

"I need a woman like you, Mary," he said bluntly. "You need a man like me. We both have seen enough hills. We've both had enough lonely dreaming. Life is taking what there is and making the best of it, Mary. I'm satisfied with you. I hope you can feel the same way about me."

The rag fell from her hands to the floor. She looked at him, and then away.

"Is it that easy, Ed?" she asked softly.

"No," he said frankly. "It isn't easy. I don't know about women, but a man has urges he can't always hold in the corral. It takes a man a time to adjust himself to anything that is new and that might be holding him down when he wants to go somewhere. I guess women aren't different. You've had one way of living and I'm asking you to change it. Maybe some people around here would figure that I'm being mighty noble and that you ought to leap at the chance to grab me. I don't look at it that way, Mary. I'm asking you because I want you. The trails you've ridden before don't bother me—not a damn bit. It's the one ahead, for both of us, that I'm worrying about. I've been worrying about it for a long time. I think you're the trail podner I need."

"You make it sound—convincing," she whispered.

Then she broke the mood with a smile and picked up the cloth.

"Don't talk like that again, cowboy. You're too sweet with that tongue of yours. You'll be into something you can't back out of."

"Straight talk," insisted Ed, "deserves a straight answer. You know that, Mary."

"All right," she sighed. "You can have it. Straight. I think I'm loco about another man, cowboy. Yet I wouldn't marry him if he's the last man on earth. I've had my share of knocks and I can take anything. I could live with you and be a good wife—as some people calculate wives. I could cook and clean house and raise babies. But there's a part of me you would never own. It isn't mine to give."

"You're not telling me anything I didn't already know," he said gently.

She stared into his gray eyes. "Knowing that—you still want—?"

"Why not?" he shrugged. "It seems to me we can ride together, or suffer the loneliness of separate trails."

Mary looked again, a shadow on her face.

"The cooking is all right. The cleaning is. But there is a part of marriage that calls for a different feeling. Duty sometimes isn't enough for that. How do you feel about that, Ed Kane?"

He remembered the thrill of her in his arms in the porch rocker, the sweetness of her hair in his nostrils. And he remembered also her soft murmur, "No, Ed, not tonight." There had been something between them, an understanding, a closeness that was not all sympathy on his side or appreciation on hers. His lips curved in a thin smile.

"I'm not worried about that either," he told her.

Her answer was quick. "Nor I," she said frankly.

"I just wanted you not to expect too much—too quick."

"I will be satisfied with what I get," he assured her.

"Then it's a deal," she cried.

"When?"

"You're ramrodding the outfit," Mary shrugged. But her smile belied the casual unconcern of her words.

"Then I'll come for you," he said, rising and pushing his cup back. "I got to see about some things first. Furniture and stuff like that."

"I'll be around," she promised.

There was a red spot in each cheek as she met his gaze. For a moment they both just looked. Then a slow smile broke across each face.

Kane pulled on his Stetson and clomped out of the hotel. This, he mused, would take the cake for getting engaged!

9

CARTER FOUND Calhoun Conroy in the book-lined recess which served as his office. Resolutely, without regard for the cost, Calhoun Conroy had transferred much of the picturesque comfort and luxury of his family's Carolina mansion into this rambling rock-and-frame house which sat on a wide sloping ridge, catching every breeze which came up the valley, no matter how gentle, and holding it with the genius architects of that period knew.

There were thirteen rooms in this huge house, all of them furnished lavishly. True, the carpets were threadbare in spots and the leather upholstery in Calhoun's library was spotted but, even after twenty years, here was the house that set a pattern for luxury and comfort in the West. Calhoun was still proud of it, as he was proud of everything the Conroys possessed.

He was a big man, more than six feet in height, dark jowled, dark eyed. As a young man he had fought with Johnston, and had fought well. The war to him had been a grievous calamity, a callous destruction of his world by a barbaric people who resented what they could not attain themselves. He had been well named, for in his bitterness and his vitriolic defiance he was as antagonistic as had been the senator for whom he was named—the John C. Calhoun who fought the South's battles with every stinging word and rasping tone in a seemingly unlimited repertory.

Calhoun had known love once. That had been too long ago. His capacity for a genuine wholesome affection had been killed by his incessant urge to establish again, in a land unmarked by his kin's graves, the inherent fact that men are not created free and equal, that some men are born with the vision and the courage to set up their clan as a superior breed. In this, Calhoun Conroy had not failed—as his own eyes saw it. The personal tragedy of his ambition had not touched him. He did not know of Catherine's wistful loneliness that at times was a stronger feeling than her inherent belief that, as the daughter of Calhoun Conroy, she lived on a plane above the valley girls and boys with whom, by sheer necessity, she must sit in school and dance at parties. He had no inkling of Davis' deep full love for Mary McGee, or the gnawing resentment in his son's heart that the girl who had given herself to other valley men must deny him because he was a Conroy.

He would have sympathized with neither. He would have said to Davis, recalling the mistresses the friends of his youth had kept in Charleston: "Sleep with her if you feel like it. It's all right to sleep with white trash. Set her up in the hotel. But don't go mooning around over a cheap woman."

Perhaps, if asked, he himself would have presented the proposition to Mary. And would have been aghast at her curt refusal.

As for Catherine—what more could any woman ask? She ruled over the biggest and loveliest and most expensive home she had ever seen. She could send to San Antonio for her clothes, or beyond. She had her own team of horses and it was her own fault if she chose to ride astraddle like a man, instead of sitting back in a carriage like a queen.

The women Calhoun Conroy had known in his youth had wanted no more.

Jefferson, lounging in the other leather upholstered chair, was a replica of him, as tall and as dark and as hot-eyed. Calhoun could guess at the motives which sent Jefferson riding in San Antonio. The drafts on Calhoun's account at the Southwest Bank of Commerce were huge, but Calhoun never reprimanded his oldest son. He had raised his children like that—to demand, and expect, anything they wanted. Though the Crown ranch was always teetering between prosperity and sheer bankruptcy, never quite touching either level, Calhoun did not raise his eyebrows at any draft which came to him by mail for his approval. His children had the right to expect all the money they wanted.

Yet he knew the weaknesses of his children. He knew that Jefferson was hot-tempered and incompetent as a foreman, that the Crown riders would have ridden away without notice had he put Jeff in charge. He knew that Davis was too amiable and lacked drive.

He did not complain. There could be no complaints against a Conroy.

Carter Slade was the foreman he wanted, and to Carter he turned for management of the ranch, which he did not feel a man of his position should do personally. Carter was the efficient overseer any plantation should have—the type of man who would have been eagerly sought after by pre-war planters in Carolina. For Carter was not only capable and hard-working, but knew his place socially. Had Calhoun known that his foreman had proposed marriage to his daughter that very morning, he would have quirted Carter then and there, as the stocky foreman stood in the library and urged upon Calhoun and Jefferson the necessity of dealing with Ed Kane.

"I don't reckon," Slade said, "that the range he is taking from us is too important. Least not this year. We got good rains and, if we have to, we could run stock in the south flats. But I've run this ranch on the theory that any affront to the Crown, no matter how trivial, was grounds for war. I ran eight or ten of Kane's steers back across the river today."

Calhoun grunted with satisfaction. That was the way the Crown should be run. He congratulated himself again on having the right man for the job.

Carter's eyes gleamed triumphantly. What a pompous old goat! It would be worth a small fortune to let Calhoun know that the Crown was being used as a pawn in Slade's game, that the Conroy hauteur and grimness of purpose were something Carter could use to hide his own motives.

Four sets of dueling pistols hung over Calhoun's desk. He eyed them fondly.

"We haven't ridden up the valley in a long time," he said. "Henry Kane was a different man—he knew his place. I haven't forgotten the side Ed Kane took during the trial."

"Aw, Pa, we settled that," broke in Jefferson, a

grin curving his thick, full lips. "Peck Purdy tended to that for us."

Calhoun's face darkened. For two days he had not mentioned to his son, Davis, that it was not in keeping with the Conroy traditions to run from a fight, especially from a shriveled little nobody like Tommy McGee.

An account of the argument, and his son's cowardice, had been given him by Carter, who naturally failed to include himself in the list of those who had backed down before Tommy's challenge.

"When do you want to visit Kane?" he asked of Carter. "And do you want to burn him out?"

"I think we had better get rid of him," Slade said hesitantly. "He's no nester. He won't watch his house and barn burn and then melt off in the brush. Kane is a gunman. Folks say he was the best gun-slick the Rangers ever had."

"Then kill him," Calhoun snapped. "Set his house on fire and shoot him down like a dog when he runs out. That should be a lesson to these valley people to leave Crown grass alone."

"They need it," Jefferson nodded. "I wanted to tie into 'em after the trial."

"If it's all right with you, Mister Conroy," Carter said in that pretended humbleness of his, "we'll go across the river tonight."

"I have no objections," Calhoun nodded.

He pondered a moment and reached into his desk

for a cigar. He handed one each to Carter and Jefferson.

"Where's Davis?" he finally asked of his other son.

"Around," grunted Jefferson. "You want him?"

"Yes. I think I shall order Davis to lead the attack on Kane."

"Pa, that ——!"

"Hush!" broke in Calhoun. "Don't speak of your brother like that. He's a Conroy."

Jefferson grunted but was otherwise silent. No love was lost between the two sons of Calhoun Conroy. They were as different as day and night, and their boyhood had been spent in petty quarrels that several times had produced an actual exchange of blows. There would have been more fights had not each trembled at the thought of the punishment that awaited them, without regard as to who had started the trouble. Calhoun Conroy had worn out more than one hackberry switch on his two boys. Then he had used his Army belt.

After he had glared Jefferson into submission he ordered: "Go get him."

Davis was talking to Catherine upstairs. "The Mister wants you," Jeff said surlily.

Davis nodded. He had expected this. In fact, he had been expecting it for two days. He had worked himself into such a state of anticipation that he sighed in relief that the summons had finally come.

Jeff walked ahead of him with no word of explanation. There was nothing between the two brothers except their different personalities—for a long time they had treated each other with a restrained courtesy. Calhoun could keep them apart but he couldn't make them like one another.

Reaching the library, Davis spoke to his father and gave Carter a surly, accusing glare.

"What's this I hear about you backing down before Tommy McGee?" barked Calhoun.

That was like Calhoun—not to waste time getting to the point.

"I wouldn't draw on him," Davis admitted. "If that's backing down, I reckon I did."

Calhoun's breathing was hard and fast. "You're the first Conroy ever to turn his back on a fight," he snarled.

Davis shrugged his stooped shoulders. "I don't guess I'm much of a Conroy," he conceded.

"I don't see how you can be a Conroy at all," sneered his father. "To let a good-for-nothing tramp like Tommy McGee back you down. He's riffraff and his father and mother are riffraff. His sister is the town whore. And *you* let him slap your face and run you out of a saloon!"

Davis had turned pale, for an obvious reason. His father mistook rage for cowardice. "And now you're trembling like a spotted pup!" he shouted. "I'm a good mind to see if I can whip some guts into you. You're not too big for me, young man."

"I wouldn't try it if I were you," Davis said slowly. His eyes were twin dagger-points. Had Calhoun not called Mary a whore, he probably could have railed at Davis for hours without meeting opposition. But Davis Conroy was a young man in love, and no filial respect can overcome that.

"I'll give you one more chance," declaimed Calhoun. "One more chance to prove you're a Conroy and a man. Tonight we are going to burn out Ed Kane and shoot him down—in his own bed, if necessary. The man who slapped your face rode for him. Kane stood against the Crown when McGee was tried. Kane is daring to run his stock across the river.

"Ordinarily," Calhoun went on, breathing hard, "it would be Carter's job. But you need to prove to this valley that you aren't a yellow sheep dog. Take the boys after dark and go over to Kane's."

Davis listened in stunned amazement. This was nothing new for the Crown. Fully half the grass they used had been won in such a manner. But not for long years had any outfit in the valley actually gone to war, and such brutal war, over government range. The unwritten and unspoken truce between the Crown and the upper valley had been rigidly observed by both sides.

Now his father proposed to break it. Ed Kane, the tall, slim man Davis liked, was to be the first victim.

Davis could see beyond this single raid. The upper valley outfits would take it as an omen of what was to come. Not all of the shooting in this valley had been done by Crown riders. Calhoun had won the fight before, at least the compromise he sought, by bringing in gunmen from San Antonio and beyond. There were three or four riders on Crown horses now who were gun-slicks first and waddies second.

Davis took a deep breath. "I don't believe in things like that," he said slowly, "and I won't have any part in it."

There were three simultaneous gasps. Then a snort of indignation that could have come only from Calhoun. The old man's face turned purple in rage. Nobody, much less his son, had dared to talk back to Calhoun Conroy! He sputtered.

"You whelp! You cowardly whelp! You ungrateful—!"

"Because you are my father," Davis said coldly, "you can talk like that and get by with it."

Another sputter.

"Get out!" yelled Calhoun, leaping from his chair.

Davis turned to go.

"I don't mean just out of this room!" stormed Calhoun. "I mean off my land. Out of my life. I never want to set my eyes on you again. To think that I've lived to see a cowardly sneaking Conroy."

"Who doesn't believe in ganging up on one man,

burning his house at night and killing him," Davis snapped.

He was not altogether without the Conroy temper. And he had taken a lot already.

"If you're so brave," he sneered at his father, "call Ed Kane out. He'll meet you."

He swung upon Carter Slade. "That goes for you too, Slade. No one ever heard of *you* shooting it out face to face with any man. Why don't you go gunning for Kane yourself?"

"You get out," panted Calhoun, trembling as he stood. "You're a Conroy and I won't see you starve. I won't see you work for another man with your hands, though you're as common as any white trash I ever looked upon. The lower valley across the river is yours. The cattle over there are yours. Take them and make the most of it. Live over there with the scum of Cotulla County. But, damn your cowardly soul, if you ever set foot on this side of the river, I'll have you shot down on sight. Tell the boys that, Carter. Tell 'em to shoot first and to ask questions later."

"Yes, sir," Slade heartily agreed. This was one command which would be promptly and enthusiastically carried out.

"That suits me," Davis muttered through tight, white lips.

He turned and walked away, leaving Calhoun still ranting. He didn't even go upstairs for more clothes. He walked straight through the corridor to the corral, saddled his horse and rode at a gallop toward the small, insignificant portion of the Crown empire that was his.

Even while he shook with anger, he was happy over the showdown. Gladly would he trade his heritage as a son of Calhoun Conroy for the few sections of canebrake and sparse bluestem across the river, where the lowland slopes turned somersaults in their haste to become a part of Sunset Rim.

He was leaving nothing behind that he wanted. Ahead of him was everything he desired—freedom from his father's tyranny, from Slade's sneers, from the narrowness and the shallow bitterness that was the Conroy stock-in-trade.

A smile broke across his dark face as he realized that at last he had something tangible to offer Mary. He had been ordered away from home—he could marry whom he pleased. And the deserted line cabin where they had met only a short time ago could be rebuilt into a cottage that would do for a time, until he sold his spring cattle.

EVERY EVENING meal at the Crown was at least a semiformal occasion. Calhoun would have liked it more so—to have had neighbors partaking of his hospitality, to have beamed down upon them with friendly condescension from his place at the head of the table. But no dinner guests were available in this new raw land. At times Carter was invited to leave the bunkhouse. Slade always accepted meekly, hating the patronizing tone in which the invitation was issued, yet accepting it until such a time as his plans could mature.

Formal dress was not required, of course, but Catherine was sternly forbidden to come to the table in her riding clothes and both boys must shed their work garments, if they had been wearing them at all that day. Calhoun had not forbidden the latter but he had discouraged it since making Carter foreman. There was no work for the boys to do, so why should they make a pretense of doing any at all? No Conroy should be required to work for a living. Only the ruthless tyranny of the damn Yankees had made it necessary for Calhoun ever to show enterprise and business judgment.

Catherine was a moment late and her father glared at her in disapproval. Carter sat across from her with Jefferson. At first she thought Davis was simply late again—usually he was the tardy one. But then she noted there was no plate set for him.

"Where's Davis?" she asked innocently.

She had heard angry voices downstairs but so often Calhoun lost his temper and stormed at his sons or his foreman that she had paid no attention to it. From her upstairs window she had watched Davis ride away, but that was not unusual either.

Calhoun was carving the roast. He laid down the heavy knife and fork and his bushy eyebrows were low and straight as he stared at his daughter.

"You are never to mention that name again," he

told her with a quiver to his tone that showed his grimness of purpose. "You are to forget that you ever had such a brother."

Catherine paled. Davis was her favorite. With Jefferson she maintained a frigid politeness. She wondered as to the details, and would not wait long to learn. She hoped that Davis had stood up to the Mister and had given him back as many hot words as he had taken.

"If you will explain where he has gone," she said coldly, "and set my curiosity at ease for once, I will try to gratify your wish."

"He has taken the lower valley land across the river," Calhoun grated. "I will send him a deed to it. The cattle over there are his. Now does that answer your question?"

"Completely," Catherine snapped, and turned her attention to her meal.

She could not eat with an appetite, however. She toyed with her food, waiting for her father to satisfy his appetite. Calhoun was a prodigious eater—of late years he had been bothered again and again with indigestion. It was a rule at the Conroy table that no one was to stir until he had finished. This had set hard with them in their earlier years, when they had been anxious to wolf their food and get in an additional hour of play outdoors before the sun set. Now they were used to it.

Catherine was more impatient than usual and it seemed to her that her father took longer. Davis had ridden away with no more than the clothes on his back. None of their men had used the line cabin in a long time—there would be no food there, no blankets, no towels. As soon as Calhoun pushed back his chair, Catherine hurried upstairs to Davis' room and began to pack his personal belongings.

Then, with the assistance of Theresa, their Mexican cook, she filled a wooden apple box with supplies—coffee, sugar, salt, pepper, a small frying pan, a small Dutch oven, a coffeepot. Theresa helped her carry the box and Davis' clothes to the corral, where she ordered one of the men to hitch a team to the buckboard.

Calhoun saw her from the front porch and beckoned to her.

"Where do you think you're going?" he demanded.

"To carry Davis his clothes," she said boldly. "And some things from the kitchen."

Calhoun started to erupt in rage, then caught himself. "Get everything of his out of the house while you're about it," he snapped, and turned away.

By whipping the team, she was able to reach the line cabin before dark. She found Davis sitting by a fire in the open, a cigarette in his mouth and a gleam in his eyes she had never remembered seeing before.

"Hi, sis. Whatcha got for me?"

Between Davis and Catherine was a relationship

not unlike other brother-sister affections. He had known immediately upon sighting the buckboard and recognizing the driver that Catherine was bringing him clothes, blankets and food.

She turned to his fire. He was roasting venison over a crude spit.

"I was afraid you would starve," she smiled, "but I guess not."

"As a matter of fact," Davis drawled, "I think I'm gonna like my exile. I've been over here three hours and I'm not tired of the peace and quiet yet."

"As a matter of fact," returned Catherine, stepping inside the cabin, "I think I envy you. If you would just clean up a little, I wouldn't mind joining you in disgrace."

"It could be," he grinned, "that I'll have somebody to clean her up before long."

"A girl, Davis?" his sister asked quietly.

"What else?"

"Anyone I know?"

"Yes."

"Who? I'm dying to know. You've sure kept your secret."

"You wouldn't like it if I told you," Davis shrugged, a shadow crossing his face.

"I don't know about that," Catherine said piqued. "I'm not as high-and-mighty as my brother and father."

"Then it's Mary McGee."

"Mary McGee! But, Davis, she—"

"Yeah, I know," he said wearily. "It's my affair, isn't it?"

"Yes, it is," she admitted quickly. "I was just surprised, that's all."

"The Mister will be surprised, too," he said bitterly. "He'll probably commit suicide when I marry her."

"Have you asked her yet?"

"Yes. She wouldn't have me."

"That would sure make the Mister want to kill himself," Catherine said with a wry smile.

"I think I can talk her into it though," Davis said, his face brightening. "Before, I didn't have anything to offer her."

Catherine sat down and laughed.

"What's so funny?" Davis demanded, ready to be angry.

"How that would sound to the Mister?" she gasped. "Before, you didn't have anything to offer her! Nothing except the Conroy position and a third-interest in the Crown!"

A grin curved Davis' lips. "It does sound funny," he admitted. "But it's the truth, Katy. If the Mister lives up to his promise to give me this spread of mesquite and canebrakes outright, I'm my own master. Think of that!"

"I have," she sighed. "I was heartbroken for you at first. But you're better off. I guess it's the only way of escape there was."

Davis turned his venison. "Doesn't that smell

good! Come over here for a square meal whenever you get hungry. No gleaming tablecloths and silver heirlooms, but clean sweet air and peace and quiet. I'm not going to town for days, Katy. I'm gonna get my fill of this freedom first."

His sister sighed again. "And if you really love Mary—I hope she will take you up, Dave. And she's crazy if she doesn't."

"You'll—speak to her, Katy, if she does—marry me?"

"Why, certainly."

"Then you're the first broad-minded Conroy I ever saw."

"I'm changing," she admitted, staring off beyond the fire. "I guess, Dave, I've fallen in love myself."

"Katy! Who with?" he cried, as delighted in his turn.

"Ed Kane—I'm afraid."

"Kane!"

He leaped to his feet. "Katy, I just remembered. That was why the Mister ran me off. They're going to burn Kane out tonight, Carter and the boys. The Mister wanted me to take the lead and I wouldn't."

"Burn Ed?"

"Yes, and kill him. Carter says he was running stock across the river and the valley people needed a lesson."

Catherine also leaped up. "We must stop them, Dave."

"We couldn't do that," he grunted. "But maybe

we can warn Kane. I should have done it on my way down here. I don't know why I didn't think about it."

"Lend me your horse," she begged. "I'll never get there in time with the buckboard."

"Sure."

She was already in the saddle before he had granted permission. "Bring him here," he called after her. "Nobody would ever think of looking for him here."

10

SLEEP CAME SLOWLY to Ed Kane. There were so many things to think about. Here he had lain last night while Mary McGee slept on his bed. And this day, acting on a strange impulse, he had asked permission from Mary's father to marry her, and had secured from her a grudging consent. It was an odd engagement. But, looking back, he did not regret it.

He did not believe in regretting what he had done, except those things he could make up for in word or deed. But he couldn't look ahead and imagine himself married to Mary, and her living here on the benchland, cooking for him and cleaning the house and making curtains to cover the dust-streaked windows. That was the test Ed Kane put to every one of his ideas. Could he picture them as already fulfilled?

He rolled over and smoked in slow deliberate puffs. Tomorrow he must ride around the valley and talk to his neighbors—Matthew Cumberland, Tolliver Winslow, Hugh Merrick and even Jeremiah Gilbert. He must show 'em the trail over the rim and how their cattle had been driven away. He must carry 'em to Black Ben's cabin and let them hear from the rustler's own lips the condemnation of a valley man, perhaps one of their number, as a cattle thief. Then, letting Black Ben go, he would let them take action.

He could do it himself. He could deal with Black Ben on his own and ride back to the valley and, with the sheriff or without, bring the right man to justice. But Kane wanted to be only a figurehead in this vengeance. He wanted to let the valley know that he was concerned only in the guilty man's punishment, regardless of his identity.

The Crown was undoubtedly implicated. Who? Kane thought again of Peck Purdy, and yet he didn't like this idea. He couldn't figure Purdy as a silent leader. Most men who lived by their guns were essentially honest. Purdy might drive off stolen cattle for another man but it was doubtful if the lean gun-hawk would steal of his own initiative.

Kane kicked off the cover and pulled on his boots. Automatically he buckled on his gun and cartridge belt and walked outside. For another night sleep would not come to him. He heard the whinny of a horse in the corral and walked in that direction. He threw extra hay into the bin and started back to the house.

Then he heard the scuff of horses above the steady rustle of the night breeze and stood still, concealed by the shadows of the corral fence.

The riders were coming straight on. Kane listened to their swelling thunder and knew there were a dozen of them, at least. As they broke through the hackberries and bore down upon his clearing, he saw their intent, for the lead man fired a shot that went screaming toward his house, tearing into wood. Its slug tore through the frame building with a small rustling echo.

Kane cursed and pulled his revolver, wishing for his more deadly rifle. Now little yellow and purple rosettes of muzzle light began to flash from all the guns and these midnight raiders broke formation and encircled his house, firing recklessly.

Ed stepped behind the high corral fence and, half-sheltered, laid his quick fire at them. A horse grunted and a man fell. He heard curses and a voice shouting: "He's back there. At the corral."

Kane ducked along the fence and came out at the backyard while bullets thudded into dark shadows hanging onto the corral. He gritted his teeth as he heard screams of pain behind him. His horses were being cut down by the rain of lead.

He saw a fading shape running toward the barn and cracked down. This was a target he could not miss and cruelly he threw shots, taking no chances on merely winging this raider. Then he fell away from the fusillade which followed the flash of his guns and rolled backwards. He reloaded as he crawled along.

"Git the ——!" a man yelled.

Kane recognized Carter Slade's voice. He started to fire in the direction of the sound but held back.

Somebody was in the house now, kicking through it at a dead run. The lamplight Kane had left behind him when he started for the barn was killed. But then, in a moment, came another glow.

They were firing the house!

Kane watched and when the man came across the porch he dropped him like a sack of grain, seeing him fall and hearing him crash. Then he heard a rider galloping in from a back trail. He turned in that direction and shot twice—once low to hit the horse, once high in an effort to kill the rider. Perhaps he missed with his second, but the first was sure. The horse screamed and pitched and even if the rider wasn't hit, he went sailing from the saddle. Kane listened for a telltale sound but none came. If the man wasn't hit, he was smart enough to lie still.

Sparks flew from his barn. That was afire too. He heard his horses breaking for the open—at least the raiders had unlatched the gate. By the first crackle of full flames from the barn he saw two men running with heads down. He threw two quick shots at them.

One fell. Kane chuckled. The Crown was paying a good price for burning out one lone ranchman.

But the last flash gave him away. Bullets screamed around him, so many that he wondered how he could miss being hit. He fell to the ground and started rolling again. No Crown man dared to show up in the light.

"Spread out!" It was Slade's voice. "Get behind him."

Whenever Kane heard a footstep he fired in that direction. Luckily he had plenty of cartridges. He could thank his lucky stars for not having undressed when he laid down that evening—for only pulling off his boots. A horse showed up behind him, a black indistinct shape. He threw a shot at it, although he could not be sure it was a Crown mount. It could easily be one of his own.

Now there were noises around him and lead hitting the ground in every direction. He suddenly came to his feet and tore straight ahead. They had located him and were closing a net around him. This caught him off guard. He reached the first hackberry that lined the spring before a rush of lead made him drop to the ground.

The house and barn were in full flames now. He could hide behind his tree and blaze away at any target that presented itself. But he couldn't be sure of another hit.

The Crown men were firing furiously. A bullet tore through the bark of the hackberry and nicked his shoulder. For a fleeting second he saw a man he was sure was Carter Slade. It was a perfect target and he threw up his gun with a grin.

But it only clicked. Empty. He loaded feverishly, praying that target would come again.

It didn't. He waited patiently, watching the shadows into which Carter had dived. He thought he saw a shape move and raised his revolver to fire. Just then something like a huge scythe cut him off his feet at one stroke and dropped him, knees and hands, to the ground. He felt, at that moment, no pain at all. Nothing but shock and a complete lack of feeling in his left leg. Searching slugs went *thwutt* through the hackberry limbs, making him roll over and over.

Now the pain was blinding. And maddening. He crawled to his feet. The leg quivered beneath him. Blindly, madly, he emptied his revolver into the darkness around him. It would have been by purest chance if any of these shots found a target.

Then, his gun clicking again, he floundered through the hackberry thicket, crawling aimlessly, trying to reload his gun. His arms and shoulders hit the edge of the spring and, before he could stop himself, he rolled in and lost his gun in the water.

He knew he was through. With a sigh he crawled through the half-filled basin toward the mouth of the spring.

Behind him he heard shouts and more gunfire.

"Just because he ain't shooting is no sign we got him," warned Carter's gruff voice. "Take it easy—he's a slick one."

But the Crown men grew bolder. They tramped through the thickets and no challenge came. Two men passed within a yard of him. He was lying in the very mouth of the spring now, up to his ears in water, hanging on to a hackberry root which jutted out from the bank. He was too weak to pull himself up. He tried when the two Crown hunters passed him up. He could only lay there and wait—and listen.

The crackling of the flames drowned out most other noises, or were they fading into one indistinct hum in his ears? These sounds grew fainter and fainter and the rock to which he hung seemed to slide beyond his fingers. His leg was solid fire, the pain growing worse. There was, at last, no sound at all from the burning house.

Just before he drifted into a completely black world he heard a voice shouting from afar:

"The —— must have gotten away. We'll work these ridges one at a time."

CATHERINE GALLOPED away from the line cabin that was now Davis' heritage, riding hell-for-leather down the rim road and turning up the valley, racing the pony until its sides heaved from exertion.

The night wind cooled her head and, as she drew close to Kane's benchland, reminded her to use caution. This was her county. She had been raised in it. She knew its people and the way they acted. Since childhood she had listened to its stories of trickery, violence and fury until they had become a part of her thinking. Inherently she could approach the scene of the fire with the cunning of a wild creature.

The flames were lower. Kane's house, barn and corral were sputtering embers. It was not the first fire ever to burst forth at night on these valley sides. As she left the road and climbed, heedless of the catclaw and the mesquite, she saw lights twinkling in near-by houses, even as far away as Jeremiah's. She cursed the valley people for not coming to Kane's aid.

Damn them, it was their fight! They had brought him back here, hoping his reputation as a gunman would scare off the Crown, would keep Carter Slade and Peck Purdy on the other side of the river. As if any force could daunt Calhoun Conroy!

She came closer, walking her horse, following the draws where the moonlight was phantom and the shadows secure. Her calmness surprised her. She could think clearly, and act deliberately.

She saw the Crown riders going across the spring and then into the timber beyond. She could read these signs as if this were an old story to her instead of a first venture. Kane had gotten away!

She realized this with a thrill. She had known he would. Here was a man who could outthink her hot-tempered father and the pursuant but unimaginative Carter Slade. They would have to get up early and ride late to get the best of Ed Kane.

She heard Slade's voice roaring out. "Cover the timber back there. He's on foot. He can't get far."

Two riders crashed through the brush almost by her. She pulled her horse back deeper in the shadows. She smiled as she thought of what would happen if they discovered her there, if they dragged her out to face Carter Slade. She could just picture the surprise on Carter's face.

They trailed past her, on all sides of her, a dozen men riding twenty yards apart. She dropped from her horse and waited for them to disappear into the timber behind. When they were gone, and their crashing was in the dark distance, she remounted her horse and edged closer to the clearing, where by now only a few burning coals marked where a house had stood, and a barn had been thrown up. She circled the scene of the fire cautiously, again obeying an instinct she did not understand.

It was as if a hidden voice had cautioned—Slade had left a man behind. He was standing under the charred hackberry that had shaded the weary sagging gate which Kane had delayed repairing in the press of other work. Presently, this sentinel grew weary of his watch and came to life, dragging his boots toward the corral. He mounted his horse and rode close enough to Catherine for her to hear him grumble, "Oh, hell!" In a moment he, too, faded into the timber.

She thought slowly and with calmness. Ed Kane had gotten away. The Crown men were combing the timber for him. If he were found, he would be shot down like a wolf. There was no mercy in her father or her father's men.

She must reach Kane. He would need food and ammunition and bedding. And a horse. Given those, Ed Kane could either get away from the valley or he could take to the high ridges and outride and outfight anything her father could send against him. Not for a moment did Catherine's loyalty waver. It was to Ed Kane, the man she had decided she loved. Having decided, there was no point in questioning its wisdom. No human raised in this new, raw county, much less a woman, could be anything but a fatalist.

She rode in a semi-circle around the clearing, calling, "Kane, Kane!"

There was no answer.

Suddenly, out of the shadows deeper than the ones she rode, came a horse and rider. She was caught in utter surprise. She could only gasp, and then give a small cry of fright.

"It's all right, Miss Conroy," said a gentle voice. "It's me, Purdy."

She recognized the tall gunman. "Oh!" she exclaimed. She didn't know whether to be relieved or more frightened. She knew of Purdy's background and why he was on the Crown payroll. She knew he was no cowman and no worker. There were grumblings in the bunkhouse because Purdy didn't like to wield a branding iron or fix a fence. Perhaps he would run straight to Carter or her father with his story.

"You shouldn't be out here," he reprimanded her softly. "Especially you shouldn't be riding around in the dark like this. We're looking for a man. I imagine most of the other boys would have shot you on sight."

"It's my affair," Catherine answered hotly. Who was this paid killer to tell her what she should or shouldn't do?

He reined closer. "I'm only telling you for your own good," he said sternly.

"I can take care of myself."

He shrugged his thin shoulders. "Have it your own way," he said. He started off, then pulled back his horse. "If you find Kane," he said with a ghost of a smile, "get him out of the country. He's too good a man to be shot down like a coyote."

"Thanks," Catherine smiled.

Purdy tipped his hat. "If you look close enough," he said in that same gentle tone, "I think you can find him. Good night."

He melted into the gloom before she could clear her throat to ask further questions.

She stared after him. It was the first speech she

had ever exchanged with Peck Purdy. She had seen him, yes—but the daughter of Calhoun Conroy did not mingle with the Crown riders, much less the strange silent men who rode in for only a short while, and whose white, uncalloused hands plainly showed they had another calling than riding fences or forking broncs.

She knew the talk—that Purdy was a wanted man in Arizona and a gun-slick. Slade had brought him to the Crown when it was rumored that Ed Kane, the Ranger who was fast and deadly with a gun, was coming back—on Jeremiah Gilbert's side.

"If you look close enough, you can find him!" Did Purdy know where Kane was and was keeping it quiet? "He is too good a man to be shot down like a coyote!" She hesitated another moment, then remembered that Purdy had ridden out of the hackberry thicket by the spring. She pushed her horse into its gloom, again calling: "Ed! Ed! Ed Kane!"

She listened to the faint droning sounds of the night. The crickets were chirping and the wind, colder and colder with its early morning chill, brushed through the hackberries in a heaving sound, like a human's laborious breathing. She called, "Ed!" again and, in sudden inspiration, dismounted and walked ahead on foot.

In a moment his whispered answer stopped her. "Here."

It was so dim that it didn't help. "Where, Ed? It's Catherine, Ed. Call out again."

"In the spring."

She knew he was hurt. His tone was thin and faded. He might be anywhere. She plunged through the willows and almost stumbled into the water. Calling again and again, she sloshed up the shallow stream in the direction of his voice. She found him half on the bank, half in the water. She bent down and touched his face. Hot and feverish.

"Can you walk?" she asked anxiously.

"No," he whimpered. "My leg."

But even as he denied his powers, he made the effort. He ground his boots against the gravel and got one leg beneath him. But that was all.

She ran back to her horse and pulled the protesting pony into the spring. Ed dragged himself against a willow, but his wounded leg would not bear his weight. He groped for the bridle and found it. He inched himself along the shrinking horse's neck and caught the saddle horn.

"Here," Catherine cried, "I'll help you."

First he raised his good leg until it caught a stirrup. "A boost now," he said. Catherine shoved against his hips. For a moment, all his weight was against her and she thought he would fall. Then he dropped on his stomach over the saddle and lay there a minute. When he was rested, he got his legs in the stirrups and straightened. Catherine caught hold of the cantle and climbed behind him, feeling his body shift. She put both arms around his waist, and held the reins around his waist.

"Can you stay on?"

"Sure."

They went down the slope at a slow walk, and reached the valley floor. Here the Frio bed lashed crookedly, like a reclining snake, and the slopes yielded to its wishes.

"Good," he breathed. "Follow the river bed."

The gentle horse splashed through the shallow water. She gave it the reins until it reached the rim road. Then she spurred it off the route home, which the pony could have followed in a blinding snowstorm, and along the seldom-used path toward Davis' cabin.

Her brother heard them coming and ran out. Ed teetered in the saddle. Catherine slipped down and walked the rest of the way while Davis steadied the almost unconscious rider. Davis helped her carry him inside the cabin, to the dusty bunk which had not been used in a long time. She was afraid it would not hold his weight but when he dropped on it with a sigh it creaked, but it did not cave in.

Davis lit the lantern she had brought with her from the Crown and she held it over the wounded man. What she saw frightened her. Kane's eyes were coal black against the pallor of his face. Pain and chill shook him and a dull stain widened on the upper part of his left trouser leg. Water dripped from his clothes. He put the back of his hand across his eyes, shielding them from the light. She lowered the lantern and turned to find him faintly smiling.

She was a straight shape in the room, momentarily still with indecision. But she knew what had to be done and she slipped her arm beneath his wet shoulders and pulled him up. "Your clothes," she explained, stripping back his coat. He moved a little to help her but the increasing quiver of his body alarmed her and she ordered him to be still and motioned to Davis instead. Between the two of them, they unbuttoned his shirt and undershirt, working quickly and urgently. They pulled off his boots and socks and threw a blanket over him.

Davis reached beneath the blanket and pulled off the rest of his clothes. She tore one of the sheets she had brought into long strips and bathed the torn, chewed hole halfway between hip and knee. The bullet had struck at a shallow angle, smashing through the soft flesh and coming out near the knee. Blood soaked the bandages as quickly as she applied them. Davis brought cold water from the stream outside and she covered the hole with wet cloth and piled blankets on top of him.

At a word from her, Davis put coffee on to boil. When it was ready, black and unsweetened, she held Kane up to drink. Three cups went down his parched throat in hurried, feverish gulps. Then, with a sigh, he pushed her hands away and fell on the bunk. He was asleep almost immediately. Only then could Catherine relax. She poured coffee for herself.

Davis was quietly watching her.

"Now what?" her brother asked softly. "You know what the Mister will say to this."

"The Mister won't get a chance," she snapped. "I'm not going home."

Davis said nothing. He had the gift of sympathetic silence where his father and brother did not. Catherine wanted to be alone—he could see that.

"I'll roll my blankets outside," he said, and arose to carry out that intention.

His sister stopped him. "You might kiss me good night, Davis," she trembled.

With a grin he bent over and grazed her cheek with his lips. He did more than that. He caught one shoulder in his powerful fingers and gripped it stoutly.

The latter action pleased her more than the kiss.

11

SAM MCGEE was awakened by the shooting and the crackling of flames. Not a household in the valley but wasn't roused from the deep, tired sleep of early morning by the shouts, the shots and the roaring of dried pine going up in smoke. They had been awakened before—Sam McGee more often than any. Twice, in the earlier and more hectic days of the valley, he had been burned out himself, rudely awakened and sent running for shelter with no more than the clothes on his back. Once the night raiders wouldn't even wait for him to dress—and a baby had been put out into the night without even a change of diapers.

That had been Tommy, Sam mused as he lay awake and listened to the clamor—Tommy who had been buried the day before in the Sadler burial plot. His wife also stirred, wide awake.

"Who is it, Sam?" she whimpered.

"I dunno."

He got up to see. Outside the wind was strong and chill. He shivered in his underwear. Not until the flames burned higher could he know that Ed Kane was the victim—the slope of the rim was against his vision.

"Ed Kane," he called back to his wife.

"Then it's that Crown!" she shuddered. "Will they come here, Samuel?"

"Dunno."

Sam shivered again and it wasn't only the cold. Usually a burning-out crew swept on to the next place. When he had moved higher on the rim, back of the Kane benchland, he had thought himself safe from Crown maraudings. But one could never be sure.

His wife climbed out of bed. "We'll wait and see," she sighed.

With the philosophy of her kind she stirred about the cabin, gathering scraps of food and extra clothes for the kids into one bundle. Now, at least, they wouldn't be pushed out into the night without anything to eat or wear. Then, the bundle in her lap, she came and sat with Samuel. They looked silently down the rim, listened to the gunshots and saw the flames spurt up higher, then gradually die out.

Neither moved until morning, and the first whimper of awakening from the youngest. Then Mrs. McGee returned to her pokeyish, aimless stirring—breakfast this time—and Sam went striding down the rim to get a better look-see.

Below him was only charred ruins where Kane's house and barn had stood. A campfire twinkled high in the timber, another in the lowlands. Too late Carter Slade had realized that Ed Kane might have fled down the rim instead of up. Peck Purdy and a half dozen riders were combing the Frio's banks, pausing only for a hurried breakfast.

By these fires, Samuel knew Ed Kane was alive. Or at least had avoided the Crown's clutches.

He returned—to the breakfast table. The crying and whimpering babies irritated him—he a man who should have been inured to them after so many years. The coffee was too weak. The bacon was burned. He railed out at his wife and she regarded him in surprise. Never, in their long years together, had she known Sam to show temper.

After breakfast he took his ax and began to hew out cedar posts from a thicket a quarter mile from the house. This put him out over the valley—he could look down and watch the manhunt. Frequently he interrupted his chopping to study the slopes below. Now the Crown men were divided into four groups. They were tearing through every thicket patch. It seemed impossible that Ed Kane could escape them.

Other eyes were following the hunt's progress. Jeremiah Gilbert studied it closely, and knowingly. The Cumberland boys rode close to Kane's and there were hot words passed when they encountered Crown riders. But no shooting. They rode back.

Phil Mallory, high on the opposite side of the rim, friendly to the Crown if to anybody, rode to see Calhoun Conroy, and then into Cotulla. There he was greeted with stares and curious whispers of, "Have they found him yet?" There had always been an undercurrent sweeping up and down this valley. Now it was congealing. Some men were afraid, and all women. Thus far it was only a war between the Crown and Ed Kane, but there was no telling how it would spread. A range war was like a prairie fire fed by the wind—it was likely to leap clear over a fire break and tear anew through an innocent pasture.

"Have they found Kane?" Mary asked Phil, as he stopped at the hotel for coffee.

Phil was a handsome man, soft and white and neat where other range men were hardened.

Mallory's friendship with Calhoun Conroy had kept his spread in operation. He bought with Calhoun and sold with Calhoun. He had a way with women and he knew Mary from previous acquaintance.

"Why so anxious? Has Kane put his brand on you?"

Mary did not tell him that she had promised to marry Ed Kane. That was something she did not want to talk about. It would have to come as a shock. Even then there would be talk enough. She was afraid of that talk. There might be insinuations, certainly covert sneers, and it would not do for Kane to hear or see any of them.

The Winslows also came into town. The restless stirring all valley men felt would not permit their return to a routine until this was over. Purdy rode into Cotulla for trail supplies, and men stood back and let him walk between them. There could easily have been a challenge despite the reputation he bore, but Purdy's only recognition of them was a casual nod. He gave them no opening. Never had the valley possessed the reckless courage or the grim will to hurl the first challenge against the Crown.

Strangely enough, only Tommy McGee, dead and forgotten, had done that.

Sam McGee finally came into town—he could not keep away. But for him no coffee at the hotel, no fraternizing with the Cumberlands and the

Winslows. For want of another excuse, he bought more shells at the general store for his buffalo gun.

"Might see a deer," he explained lamely.

Larry Sadler shook his head. "Plenty of people are thinking about deer," the storekeeper said sorrowfully. All morning he had been selling shells. His ammunition trade was like that. Sadler, who had been a preacher in his youth, was not at all sure that he would not have to pay retribution in another world for even carrying shells in stock.

Mary, her face troubled, her eyes red, asked Jeff Cumberland the eternal question:

"Have they found him yet?"

In the saloon Jerry McGee scrubbed the bar until it shone. The display of energy went unnoticed. His customers would not have cared if dust laid on it an inch thick.

It was no affair of his, Jerry was thinking. He didn't care. It was the place of a McGee to keep his mouth shut.

Fats Haley, who owned the bar, stepped out into the street. Jerry gulped a glass of straight whisky.

At the Crown ranch Calhoun ordered coffee brought to his library. He sipped it slowly, looking out of the window over the rolling valley. Jefferson stalked in, gun swinging low at his hip.

"The buckboard is still at Davis'," he growled. "Guess she musta stayed there all night."

Calhoun nodded. "If she wants to stay over there," he said slowly, biting each word, "she's as welcome as hell. If she ain't got any more gumption than to turn her back on a good home, she isn't worth fooling with."

Jefferson nodded, a sneer on his lips.

"They still haven't found Kane. Slade sent three men high up on the rim. But nobody can figger how he could get away on foot."

"He's somewhere," growled Calhoun. "Tell 'em to keep after him. I don't want 'em coming back to the ranch until they have Kane."

Jefferson nodded again. He drank coffee and rode back with the message.

He found Carter cursing over a noonday fire. Slade was a careful, methodical creature of routine. Things that upset his schedule irritated him. Even a minor incident could throw him akilter.

This was nothing minor. They had set out to get one man with all the Crown had, including a paid gunman who demanded a hundred a month just to ride with them. They didn't have Kane. They had burned his home and fired a hundred or more shots at him and they knew he was still free in this valley, laughing at their efforts to track him down.

Carter took out his spleen on Purdy.

"I thought you were a man-hunter," he snarled at the tall gunman.

Purdy stirred his black camp coffee. "Mostly," he said dryly, "my experience has been the other way."

"I don't see how you figger you're worth what

we're paying you," Carter complained. "I never saw a sorrier fence hand. And, when the showdown comes, you ain't any better than we are."

"You offered me the job," shrugged Purdy. "Reckon you can pay me off any time you aren't satisfied."

Carter could not know what Purdy was thinking—that the thin man would relish his discharge from the Crown. Purdy did not know why he didn't quit of his own initiative. He did not relish this ganging up. He had nothing but scorn for Carter Slade and for Calhoun Conroy who had ordered it. The job was not important to him. He had a month's pay in his pocket and he had drifted before. But something held him back. He would not have thought of it as loyalty.

Had Slade been smarter, he would have withdrawn the Crown riders and ordered Purdy to track down Kane alone. But Carter couldn't know that this was the way to handle a man. He wanted to give the orders on the hunt himself, and Purdy let him. Nor did Purdy call to Carter's attention tracks in the river bed that told him—who had been so careful with his own trails that he knew how to read others—that along here a horse had plodded recently, carrying a double burden. Purdy could even put two and two together and guess where Catherine had carried the wounded man.

Carter didn't even know Kane had been hit, hadn't noticed the blood spots in the hackberry clump. Purdy had. Furthermore, Purdy knew that Davis had been ordered away and that his sister had driven over in the buckboard with personal effects and supplies the night before. Not many things happened that Purdy's mildly inquisitive eyes didn't notice.

Had he been asked directly about these things, he would have given a direct answer.

They wolfed their meal and Slade ordered them into the saddle again. They knew their foreman—there would be no rest until they had found Kane. There was no rest ever until the job Carter assigned to them was finished. He was a patient man in his planning, and a shrewd one, but in carrying out his plans he was sometimes guilty of impatience. Each task had to be accomplished and out of the way so that he could plan another.

They spread out over the range, twenty yards apart. Their hunt covered grass used by the Winslows and the Cumberlands. Carter neither stopped nor estimated the results of this trespassing. His was a one-track mind.

But in town, sitting glumly, watching and waiting, it was discussed. The Winslows and the Cumberlands stood in one cluster before the saloon and when Jeremiah Gilbert rode up they gave him sidewise looks. Tolliver Winslow, the white-haired, seventy-year-old man who still ruled his clan with a hand of iron, stopped whittling and raised his bushy eyebrows.

"The Crown," said Jeremiah, "is getting too danged big for its britches."

Anxiety was hidden beneath his sparse whiskers and sharp shrill voice. Carter had sent him word that Ed Kane had stumbled upon the hidden pass over the rimtop. Except for Kane, Jeremiah would have gloated in the present conflict, and would have been quick to seize upon the manhunt as an excuse to launch his long-planned attack upon the Crown. But until Kane was out of the way, his hands were tied.

Sam McGee came into this group, his faded eyes harder and more level than men had remembered seeing them. Some of his hang-doggishness was gone. He stood right up among them and gave each man a nod in greeting.

"If you ask me," he grated, supplementing Jeremiah's words, "it's time something was done about the Crown."

"Nobody asked you," growled Tolliver Winslow, looking away.

"Then I'm saying it anyhow," said Sam, sticking out his chin. "Ed Kane is a white man. He's the whitest man this valley ever saw."

His voice raised itself in pitch. "You men wanted him there on the benchland," he accused them. "You, Jeremiah Gilbert, wrote him to come back. Oh, I heard the talk that went around. Get Ed Kane back here and the Crown will be afeard to come across the river. Well, they ain't afeard.

They hired themselves a gun-slick and came splashing over. And what does Ed Kane's friends do? They hide in town, drinking likker in a cheap saloon. You got him here to fight your battle for you, but you ain't got the guts to stand up with him."

"Shut up!" snarled Keith Cumberland, pushing him heavily.

Sam McGee tottered and almost fell. Other men had pushed him, some of these same men here. Tolliver Winslow had once given him a severe whipping. Sam had never stood up to them.

He pulled himself up and glared at the towering Cumberland.

"You're a bigger man. You're a younger man. You can push an old man like me around and nobody can stop you. I ain't got a friend to step to my side. You know that, else you wouldn't have done it."

"Listen, McGee," growled Keith, "I don't want trouble with you. You're an old man, but that don't give you any call to lay a man out before his friends. Now if you don't want to get licked, get out of here and shut up."

"Let me finish what I got to say," Sam insisted with a strange fearlessness. "You can push an old man around all you wanna. Your friends here, including your brothers, will think that's funny. Maybe you get a kick out of it yourself."

As a breathless hush fell upon the circle of men, he stepped forward and jabbed Cumberland's chest with his finger.

"But what I wanna know, Cumberland, is whether you got the guts to ride with a helpless old man against the Crown?"

A deeper hush. "What do you mean?" Keith asked finally, his face a lighter shade.

"Just what I said!" shrilled Sam. "The McGees have been white trash around this valley a long time. We've been kicked and pushed from one side to the other. You've all done it. I've heard you, Tolliver Winslow, call us yellow rats. Well, what about it? Who'll ride with old Sam McGee against the Crown?"

Jeremiah studied their faces. Sam had leaped in where he feared to tread. For a long time Gilbert had been wondering how he could whip up their spirits to such a height. Here old Sam McGee had done it.

He stepped in. McGee must not take the leadership away. McGee must not rush them into a rash move.

"Come down to my office," he suggested. "We'll talk some. I think Sam has something."

Uneasy glances passed. Matthew Cumberland and Tolliver Winslow looked questioningly at each other.

Jeremiah solved their indecision. "Sam is right," snapped the owlish little banker. "Anybody who ain't a blamed coward don't need a second invitation."

Matthew and Tolliver exchanged nods. Their big brawny sons were right behind them as they followed Jeremiah down the street to the bank. Their faces were aglow with anticipation. They had waited a long time for this. Indecision, rather than fear, had held them back before. They had known the Crown was too big for one man, or one family, to tackle. But if the entire valley was going to ride—count them in.

Ahead of them marched Samuel McGee, his eyes shining with a purpose. Why shouldn't he be right in the van? Hadn't Ed Kane asked, like a gentleman, to marry his daughter?

Behind them Fats Haley walked into the saloon shaking his head.

"There's going to be trouble," he muttered, pouring himself a drink.

"Danged fools," grumbled Jerry. "They'll be shot to pieces."

Fats finished his drink and regarded the scrawny little bartender with sudden distaste.

"If you was half a man," he grunted, "you'd ride with 'em. Ed Kane gave your brother a lift. Stood with him in the street when nobody else had the nerve. Your pappy was right in the bunch. How come it ain't your fight, too?"

Jerry McGee paled. His fight? Him a fighter? Then he saw again a picture that had bobbed in and out of his mind these past days. A slight little chap standing up to Davis Conroy, slapping his face, sneering at Carter Slade, turning on his heel and swaggering out of the saloon with all the arrogance of a bantam rooster. And diving for his gun against Peck Purdy—ill-advised perhaps, but unafraid.

"Lend me a gun," he whispered.

Then he realized what he had said. "No, no, no!" he shouted. But Fats was pushing a gun in his hands.

"Pour yourself a stiff drink," said the saloon owner. "And watch that gun—the safety is loose."

As the men walked along, Jeremiah was saying: "We gotta use our noodle about this. Right now ain't the time."

12

CATHERINE SLEPT ONLY at shallow intervals, constantly wakened by Kane's restless turning on the bunk, by the impact of pain on his breathing each time he tried to shift the weight of his leg. Placing her hand along his cheek, she could feel its coldness. Once in the long hour before daylight he asked for water, and afterward fell back into solid sleep.

It didn't last long. Throughout the morning, he drifted in and out of small periods of half-sleep. At those times when he was awake she laid her hand on his chest and held it there, her lips and eyes trying to help him. Always he was conscious, but always silent, except for a faint smile.

His wound was not serious. It was the loss of blood which had weakened him. She continuously changed the bandages and the swelling and the purple tint disappeared rapidly. By noon he had conquered the fever and was able to think and talk clearly.

Davis brought in a fresh-killed fawn and the broiled tender meat was just what Kane needed. He ate sitting up, now fully aware of what went on around him and able to ask where he was and how he had come there. When she explained, he studied her a moment, as if in surprise, and then looked away.

Now Davis bent over. "Sorry about last night, Kane," he mumbled, awkward with his apology. "Don't hold Catherine and me responsible for everything the Crown does."

It was not in Kane to feel bitterness. He could even understand the Crown's viewpoint—to a certain extent. That was life in this country—a fight for grass. He had been raised in the unreasonable prejudice against Calhoun Conroy that the valley people felt, but, riding away and seeing and knowing other range hogs, he had decided that the top dog wasn't to blame. There was only so much grass and every man wanted to run more cattle. The grass he coveted must naturally be his neighbor's. In the same vein, his neighbor coveted his. A gun was the only answer to such a difference. In other places a new kind of law had taken over and was satisfactory. Here in the valley such law was still only a temporary concession to what men knew deep in their hearts was right, but which they didn't want to admit had come. None of them wanted it, except inasmuch as it restricted his neighbor.

Ed Kane had represented that law—a law nullified by a people's unwillingness to accept an impersonal fairness, by their insistence that life and death, particularly life, was a very personal problem. He knew the slowness of law, and its limitations.

Kane grinned at Davis and Catherine and refused to discuss the fight, except to look wonderingly at Catherine. Kane was no wiser about women than any other man. The last time she had seen him, she had surrendered to his lips, and then had broken away from him with expressions of hatred. He could not know that a woman, like this frontier breed, opposed a change from an automatic instinct that went farther back than Ed Kane, or Catherine Conroy. Like men, women find it difficult to surrender to a new kind of law.

He ate again in a couple of hours. He was ravenously hungry. With no infection in his leg, with the bullet hole in flesh that would heal quickly, he was staging a marvelous recovery.

Davis rode off after this second meal and

Catherine was alone with Kane, who slept again, now peacefully and restfully. When he awoke the sun was setting over the rimtop and he asked to be helped outside in the cool. He limped along with the help of her shoulder.

"You're tough as leather, Ed Kane," she laughed. "You'll be up and about in no time."

He settled against the trunk of a Spanish oak and rolled a cigarette. It helped him. A physique like his, hardened by long hours in the saddle, would throw off such a wound in short order. Already he was feeling restless, and wondering if his bad leg would prevent him from sitting a horse.

And yet, in a startlingly quick transition, he felt a strange peacefulness. Perhaps it was the changed nature of the girl beside him. He could never remember her as calm and soothing. Even her beauty was of the stormy type, with her hair trailing off in the slightest breeze and her clothes that always set off the swells of her body. He had reflected previously upon the strangeness of her and Mary. Catherine's beauty was sensuous and pagan, Mary's quiet and docile. One should have been the other, and vice versa.

"What are you thinking of, Ed?" she whispered.

"You," he answered immediately.

Since mid-morning, and the disappearance of his fever, Catherine had been very thoughtful. The realization that she had practically thrown herself at this man had thrilled her, and yet dismayed her.

It was not in a Conroy's nature to be doubtful of what a Conroy proposed to do, yet before this gray-eyed man one Conroy fury and purpose had failed. So might another.

"What about me?" she demanded.

Yes, indeed, what about her? She had rescued him from the very clutches of Carter Slade, her father's foreman. What was that? Was it a proposal? She had chosen to thrust off the shackles of her people and to stand at his side. Her stealth had not been shame, but sheer necessity. Were Carter Slade, even her father, to ride into this clearing she would fight for Ed Kane to their faces, even to their deaths. Did he know that or should she tell him? And, if he did know it, what did it mean to him? He had caught her and kissed her but Catherine knew enough of the ways of men to give this rash, impulsive gesture its true value. She was attractive, yes. Any man would want to kiss her. And more.

She could not understand her own submissiveness—she, too, was that young and inexperienced. Until a certain point is reached, a woman is the master of a man. He is hers until she makes her decision, and then the tables are turned. She is in his hands, since the last weapons she has to use against him have been thrown away. At least, that is so in a land that is by harsh, grim necessity a man's land.

She was as helpless before Ed Kane as he had

been before the attack of her father's crew, without even the defiance that Ed Kane could show and carry on, even in defeat.

"What about me?" she asked again, when he was slow to answer.

"I was thinking," he murmured, "what a charming girl you are. In man talk, you're a good hand to ride the river with."

"Thank you," she murmured, angry at herself for being so grateful for his compliments. How could the daughter of Calhoun Conroy be so meek before a man?

"You will make," he went on in that same musing tone, "some man a good wife. I used to pity the man who would marry you. I used to think that the man who got you would have to keep a blacksnake handy. And a padlock, too. You're sweeter without that Conroy temper, Catherine."

She looked away. Was this all he intended to say? She waited. Surely he must realize that in this land a girl could not make second decisions. Once her mind is made up, the aftermath is inescapable, without side trails leading off into other valleys. There was nothing for her now but Ed Kane. Even if she had not realized she loved him, that was so. Often such decisions—and such marriages—were reached without the culmination of love. Too often love was a luxury, and a delay, that the swift tempo of this land could not afford and would not wait for.

She turned. He was looking up at her through half-closed eyes. Her glance roved over him—his unshaven lean face with its dark stubble. She felt a sudden wild urge to rub her cheeks against that stubble until it brought blood. She suddenly realized she had never felt the roughness of a man's beard on her face. Not even as a little girl, for Calhoun Conroy's early-morning shave was a ritual. And the father's neatness and orderliness had been passed on to his two sons.

Had he not smiled, she might have withheld herself. But he did smile, and the sharpness left his eyes and the sternness of his face relaxed. With a little cry she bent and kissed him.

For a tingling, delicious moment she felt his response, wild and upsurging. Then she sensed his reserve. He did not move.

He did not need to move. The inherent wisdom that is every woman's rushed to her rescue. She raised up, and looked away. She stood, trying to make her voice even.

"Never mind, Ed," she said. "It was an accident."

"Our second," he said gravely.

"Oh, well," she shrugged. Her hair tossed with the motion and fell over her shoulders.

"You're a wonderful woman, Catherine."

His soft voice floated up to her. She wanted to scream out at him at least to hold his tongue. Anything he could say would make matters only worse.

"Thanks, podner," she said lightly. "I'll see about supper. That left-over venison should make a good stew."

"I'm hungry enough to eat a bear," he grinned.

Sure he was hungry. A man always was. Life to him was that—food and sleep and, in between, secondary to either, a woman's kiss and a woman's love.

He lay back against the oak, closing his eyes. He was still exhausted. His body was limp and motionless. But his thoughts were busy. He could hear Catherine stirring inside the cabin, now emptying refuse from their dinner outside.

She had voluntarily kissed him! Her light explanation had not fooled him—it was no accident. His blood still tingled from the touch of her soft lips.

But this was a madness he would not permit to go on. It must not go on.

She came back with fresh coffee. "You'll have to admit the service is good around here," she laughed.

"Bueno," he agreed. She started back to the cabin but he stopped her with a motion of his hand.

"Catherine," he said slowly, "I never—I haven't told—you didn't know I was getting married, did you?"

There, it was out. He watched her face redden. "Anyone I know?" she asked lightly.

"Yes, Mary McGee."

"I know her," she nodded.

Her tone brought a glint into his eyes. “And you don’t approve of her?”

Catherine turned away. Back over her shoulder she said: “I don’t suppose it’s my place to approve or disapprove of the woman you marry, Ed Kane.”

Inside, over the fire, she realized for the first time what he had said. He was going to marry Mary McGee! All she had thought of when he had spoken was the rebuff his faltered explanation carried to her and her hopes. That, for the moment, had been most important.

Mary McGee! Poor Davis! Another Conroy with a broken, crushed dream.

She sat down on the edge of the bunk and cried. Kane heard her sobs from the oak tree. He swore. Where a woman cries, a man smokes and swears. He handled papers and tobacco with shaky fingers.

Davis returned before dark. There was something in his face that told Catherine he had seen and talked to Mary McGee, and that Davis had received an answer not unlike hers. She guessed correctly. Davis *had* talked with Mary. And Mary *had* told him she was to marry Kane.

Davis paced the cabin restlessly. He went outside and smoked with Kane. They talked in short, terse generalities—the weather, the floods on the Frio, the wild game on the rim heights. Davis came back inside and glowered at his sister. The stew was boiling and she was just taking it up.

"I think you had better go home right after supper," he said harshly. "This is no place for you."

"I had intended to," she agreed.

She didn't wait to eat. Kane watched in silence as she hitched the team to the buckboard. She was going. She was going back to the Crown and she would stay there. She was going back to Calhoun Conroy and she would re-learn that quick flashing temper and her eyes again would take on that stormy, untamed gleam.

"Davis will look after you until you can ride," she explained to him, not trusting herself to meet his eyes. "If I get a chance, I'll get a horse over to you."

"Thank you," he said gravely.

He felt no qualms of conscience. He had not known events would follow this queer trend. It was a break from the valley's pattern that no man could have foreseen, least of all himself.

Besides, what good was a man's conscience, or a man's regrets? This girl herself was to blame. How could she expect to be one person one day and an entirely different woman the next, completely reversing herself and her heritage, completely wiping out in one short night and day the impressions of twenty years?

Catherine whipped the team into a run. The buckboard careened dangerously over the rocky road leading back to the rim thoroughfare. Not until she had sighted the big white mansion did she meditate upon what was before her.

What if Calhoun didn't permit her to return? The Mister was fully capable of such a step. He did not tolerate disobedience. He had ordered Davis out of their lives, and meant it. His rage would reach a ferocious pitch and his words would be harshly condemning.

No riders were stirring around the corral, only Pancho, the Mexican boy.

"Where are all the men?" she asked.

"Still after Senor Kane."

"Is my father here?"

"*Si*, Senorita. Senor Jeff, he gone."

Catherine was glad of that. She would rather face the Mister's outburst than Jefferson's sneer.

She found her father in his library. He was sitting in one of the overstuffed rockers, swaying back and forth. She stepped in without a word and waited for him to begin.

He saw her immediately but looked back to the window as if she hadn't made an impression on him. Then, after a long while, he asked:

"Stay with Davis last night?"

"Yes."

"Is he fixed up all right?"

"Yes."

She held herself stiff and straight against the inevitable storm.

"I hope," Calhoun remarked, "he can make a go

of it. He and I never could hit it off. We never saw things alike. But there must be some good stuff in him. A Conroy can't be all rotten."

"No, sir," she agreed, her lips moving without communication from her brain.

Was this to be all? What had happened to the stormy petrel that had been the Mister?

"We still haven't got Kane," he said gently. "In a way, I hope he gets away. Clean away. I think I could have liked Kane."

This was the straw that broke the camel's back. Catherine turned and fled upstairs to her room in tears.

CARTER RODE BACK to the Crown headquarters for provisions and fresh horses. Catherine heard him clomping into her father's library.

"That Kane is a slick one," the foreman fumed. "We've combed every acre of brush in the valley and not a sign of him. I'm going to take the boys up on the rim and work down."

Calhoun agreed. Though he was secretly pleased and regretted ever permitting the attack on Kane, he must not—he could not—let the manhunt peter out. The Crown's prestige hung upon finding Kane and getting rid of him. It was regrettable, and if Calhoun had it to do over again he would have been willing to work out a compromise. But now the die was cast and there was no turning back. He even deliberated on whether or not he should take to the trail himself.

He decided against it. The men ate at the bunkhouse and rode out again. Some of them complained—this hunt had been going on for three days and it was like searching for a needle in a haystack. Most of them were sure that Kane was safely out of the valley, or at least had reached a friendly ranch and was in secure hiding there.

Carter barked down their objection. He ordered them to spread out and led them straight up the rim, intending to work as high as the secret pass. All along were the prints of the past three days, now singly and now in pairs, a pattern of hoofprints that told its futile story.

Although the upper valley pretended to ignore the hunt for Kane, not an eye missed a single detail of it. High up among the timber Sam McGee watched closely. At the talk in Cotulla it had been decided to fight cunning with cunning.

Jeremiah Gilbert wanted no shoulder-to-shoulder fight. "By God, the Crown don't fight that way," he argued. "They sneak up on a man at night and shoot him down, sometimes as high as twenty guns to one. We'll fight 'em the same way."

Though Tolliver Winslow and the Cumberlands and even Sam McGee would have been willing to ride over in daylight and shoot it out, they agreed to Jeremiah's strategy. McGee, suddenly a man of responsibility among them, and respected as such, was given the chore of watching the Crown riders until they disappeared up the rimside. At the first opportunity, they would swoop down on the Crown and "show Calhoun Conroy he wasn't so high and mighty."

McGee maintained a night and day vigil, munching on hardtack and dried venison, never leaving his flickering campfire. Once the Crown riders, re-working the timber, stumbled upon him. He ordered them off with a curt "none of your business and get the hell out of here" when they wanted to know why he was sleeping out. When they hesitated, he brandished his buffalo gun in their faces.

"I ain't asked you in to my fire," he screeched. "Get the hell out of here and leave a man alone."

They obeyed, although one of them sneered that he was sure talking up for a nester.

With a sneer for their bullheadedness, Sam watched Slade lead his riders away from the Crown. Jeremiah and all of the upper valley men were likewise hunting for Ed Kane, but covertly. The Crown worked as if it were out on a rabbit drive, and anything it stirred would flee straight ahead in fright. McGee waited until it was certain that Slade was heading up the rim and then he doused his fire and rode across the timber to Tolliver Winslow's. There, it had been agreed, the upper valley men would meet.

He stopped at the front gate and hailed Tolliver. The seventy-year-old man came out quickly. When

McGee explained that the Crown riders were now high up on the rim, and pointed to their fires twinkling across the emptiness as evidence, Tolliver sent his riders out to the nearby ranches, to the Cumberlands and to Jeremiah's, to the Merricks and the Picketts. All of them had been contacted and all had agreed to be represented on this cleanup of cleanups.

Tolliver had been eating. He remembered the apple pie and spareribs and turned back to resume his meal, leaving Sam still standing at the gate. Winslow hesitated. To invite a man to eat at your table was to admit him as an equal and in his thirty years in the valley Sam had never experienced the thrill of such an invitation. Tolliver thought a moment. Finally he grunted back over his shoulder:

"I'll have maw set an extra plate, Sam. Come on in."

Sam gasped. He had not expected that. Usually, when he came to see ranchmen, they calmly and deliberately finished their supper before talking to him at a back gate. Now he was walking right into Tolliver's house, through the front door. Mrs. Winslow raised questioning eyes but did not dispute her husband's order to "fix a place for Sam here."

The Winslows set a table quite in contrast with the McGees' meager fare. Spareribs, venison and beef—Tolliver lived well. He fed his drove of brawny sons until they were as broad as they were long. You could always look to Tolliver's clan for the champion bulldogger of the valley.

Before they finished, the Cumberlands came riding up. As soon as she heard their footsteps, Mrs. Winslow put an extra pot of coffee—a huge one—on the stove to boil and, with a philosophical sigh, brought two pies out of the pantry. She had probably cooked more food than any other three women in the valley, for boys and men were always trailing in to eat with her sons. And Tolliver was as bad as the boys about inviting people in on short notice.

Jeremiah galloped up right on the Cumberlands' heels. His scrawny, unshaven face gleamed with excitement.

"We'll wait till after midnight, boys," he said. "Let 'em bed down. It would serve 'em right if we burned the house right around 'em."

Jeremiah carried a rifle, no revolver. The other men wore both. Tolliver strapped on a heavy gun belt and sent for the horses. Jeremiah urged waiting. The Merricks had said they would be over.

In less than ten minutes Grady Pickett rode up. His dad and brothers, he explained, were off at line camp. Close behind, riding stiffly and cursing the gait of his horse, was Jerry McGee.

Jeremiah lifted his eyebrows. No one had believed that Jerry would be in at the finish. It was on the tip of the banker's tongue to order the bartender back to town. Then he remembered that Sam McGee had proposed this show, and there was certainly nothing about Sam's grim attitude which didn't inspire confidence.

And, after all, the more the merrier.

They drank their coffee and Tolliver's wife supplied another pie. Seemingly the Winslow larder was limitless.

They waited until nine o'clock. Then Jeremiah swung into the saddle and they rode toward the valley at a slow gait. They crossed the Frio, splashing through the shallow water.

Sam McGee and Tolliver were right behind Jeremiah. Sam's eyes shone with a queer flame. He was riding shoulder to shoulder with the valley's most influential men, Tolliver and Gilbert. When Winslow bit off a plug of eating tobacco he suggested to Sam they change places.

"Want to be spittin' downwind," explained Tolliver.

13

JERRY HUNG BACK. He still couldn't understand his presence here among these warlike men riding across the valley to burn and destroy, and to kill if there were opposition. He had no rifle, only the pistol Fats had lent him. The horse sensed his nervousness and cut up. Jerry held too tight a bit and the pony didn't like it.

They clattered up the rocky rim road. They could see Calhoun Conroy's two-story house now, a square dark shape against the shadows cast by the rim beyond. The moon ducked behind a convenient cloud, as if approving that the Crown hour had come. They drew up at the well-beaten trail leading off the main road and breathed their horses a minute.

Then Jeremiah spurred forward.

"We'll give 'em a chance to get their women out," he said.

It was a great moment for Jeremiah. For years he had dreamed of this. "The goddam little Yankee" Calhoun had threatened to horsewhip on sight was leading a dozen armed men to settle their account. For years he had nurtured a hatred of Calhoun that was almost fanatical. Calhoun had called him a "dirty, thieving little coward." The Crown had refused to bank with him, Calhoun saying he didn't "want any dirty Yankee hands on his money." Gilbert loved power and wealth, but it was hatred rather than greed which made him ride forward with his rifle out of its scabbard. It was hatred that made him itch to fight.

They encircled the lush yard, still without being challenged. Another ranch would have had watch-dogs. Calhoun couldn't stand their yapping. Here were planted honeysuckle and camellias and dozens of other shrubs which had never flowered, but which hung pitifully between life and death. There were many features of his beloved Southland that not even Calhoun's iron will could impress upon this country.

Jeremiah reined up.

"We'll fire a shot or two through the house just to show 'em what's up," he croaked. "Then we'll give 'em time to get their women out."

He threw his rifle to his shoulder and a shot screamed through the roof. It was a signal. A barrage shook the Conroy mansion, bringing Calhoun to his feet with a roar, and Jefferson running out to the second-story porch.

"What in the hell goes on here?" shouted Jefferson.

He was in his nightshirt. Behind him appeared Calhoun, his white hair shining in the pale moonlight. Catherine, likewise awake, listened for their voices.

"Get off my ranch!" yelled Calhoun down at the raiders.

Jeremiah's voice, ever shrill when he tried to lift it, floated up to the Mister.

"We'll give you ten minutes to get your daughter and other women out, Conroy. Then we're firing the place."

Calhoun trembled in his rage. Fire his place like a damned nester!

"I'll see you in hell first, you penny-pinching Yankee!"

He dived back into his room for his gun. Jefferson, saner in this dangerous moment than his father, caught the Mister's arm. "We'll have to take 'em up," said the son. "Let Catherine get out of here with her clothes."

Now she was with them, a filmy light bedroom coat thrown over her gown. "Give me a gun," she said tight-lipped. "I can fight as well as either of you."

"No," growled Calhoun. "Get dressed. Get some things in a bag. Go to town. Not Cotulla. Go across the rim to Uvalde."

"No, Dad. It's a Crown fight. Let me stay here."

"No."

"Then let me go after Carter and the boys. They're not over an hour's ride away."

The Mister hesitated, his shaggy eyebrows creased in thought. "That's your job, Jeff," he ordered. "Sneak out the back door. There are some horses in the lower pasture. Grab one and go for Carter. I'll try to hold 'em off."

"But, Dad, can't I—?" appealed the girl.

Calhoun shook his head. "This is no place for a woman. Do as you're told, girl."

Catherine went back to her room. Calhoun shouted down from the balcony.

"My daughter is dressing. She'll be out in a few minutes."

"Now," he whispered to Jeff. "They'll hold off shooting till Catherine gets clear."

Jeff nodded. He slipped into his room for his belt and gun and then stole down the stairs, pulling on his pants over his nightshirt, walking noiselessly in his bare feet. He watched from the back door a moment and saw two shadows converging upon it. A window was open off the Mister's library. He sneaked through it.

Footsteps came toward him. He froze against the side of the house. Two of the Cumberland boys swept on within a yard of him. He gripped his gun butt tightly but was not seen.

He waited a moment, then broke across the open for the shelter of an elm grove. Again he was unchallenged.

Running low, gun out, he veered around the elms. His heart thumped jubilantly.

He had made it.

JERRY MCGEE quaked as the Mister's defiant voice thundered back from the balcony. This was no place for him, Jerry thought. He had been pushed into this anyhow—Fats Haley had compelled him to ride along. He fingered the gun at his side. What the hell! If men wanted to shoot each other up, let 'em. He made a living serving drinks and he didn't bother nobody. This was no affair of his.

He shrank away from Tolliver Winslow and his father.

"Some of you men go around to the back,"

ordered Jeremiah. “We don’t want ’em sneaking out the back door.”

Two of the Cumberland boys left their horses. Jerry scrambled down.

“I’ll go with ’em,” he said eagerly.

“All right, McGee,” Tolliver said curtly.

Jerry watched his chance. The Cumberlands strode hurriedly, shoulder to shoulder, one as big as the other. Jerry trailed them a moment watching his chance and, as they disappeared, he dove into the elm grove. He would hide here until the fight was over, then he would come out and pretend that he had been in the middle of it all along. That would give him a certain prestige in town—he could say he had been in the fight at the Crown. And yet he wouldn’t be shot up fighting a battle that was never his in the first place.

He shrank back in the shelter of the elms, screened from even a wild shot.

He had been there just a moment when he heard stealthy footsteps. His body stiffened and his heart stopped beating. Godamighty! Someone was coming into the dark after him!

He twisted around until he was concealed by an elm trunk, his nervous hand clutching the butt of his gun.

The limbs in front of him parted and Jefferson stole through, his breath heavy against Jerry’s face.

Jerry moaned. A Conroy!

Jeff heard that moan. He whirled and swung at

Jerry with his gun butt, unwilling to risk a shot.

Jerry dodged. He fell backward and tripped on a root. There was a roaring as Jerry's gun went off. Jeff dived after him. Jerry pulled the trigger again and again. He kept pulling it even after the cylinders were empty.

Then he realized that the body lying half across him was limp and motionless. He pushed up with his elbows.

Somebody came tearing through the trees. It was Jeremiah.

"God dammit, who started this shooting?"

The little man was furious. His plans just couldn't go wrong now.

He helped pull Jerry up, cursing him for going off half-cocked. Then he turned over the lifeless man and recognized him.

"Gawd! Jeff Conroy!"

Jerry whimpered. He had killed a man. This thought pounded against his eardrums in a crazy rhythm. He had killed a man!

Now Tolliver ran across the yard.

"What is it?"

"Conroy, Jeff Conroy," said Jeremiah, a grin on his scrawny face. "He tried to get away. McGee here ran him down and killed him."

Tolliver stared down at the corpse, and at the trembling Jerry, in disbelief. Then he sighed as if to say, "Well, I've seen everything." He slapped Jerry's shoulder.

"Good work, McGee."

Jerry's lips twitched but he couldn't utter a sound. Finally, he laughed. It was a wild laugh. They thought he had killed Jeff Conroy on purpose. They thought he had seen a man fleeing, and had followed him into the dark of the timber and had killed him in a chest-to-chest gun fight.

As stern and unyielding as were Tolliver and Jeremiah, that laugh shocked them. Later, telling his sons about it, Tolliver would shake his head and say that he wouldn't have believed it if he hadn't seen it with his own eyes. McGee shooting down Jeff Conroy, and then laughing about it. A tough little hombre. They had figgered the McGees wrong all along.

A shout came from the front of the house.

"The Conroy gal is coming out!"

It was true. A small valise under her arm, Catherine stepped uncertainly off the porch and looked around her.

Ellis Winslow came forward.

"Better hurry, Miss Conroy. I'll hitch up a buckboard or saddle a horse, whichever you want."

Ellis had gone to school with her, had danced with her at valley parties. Once, in the long ago, he had even sparked her for a summer, riding across to the Crown ranch and sitting with her on the wide, deep front porch. She gave him a cold smile.

"Thanks so much," she said bitterly. "But I can look after myself."

A voice shouted from inside.

"All clear, girl?"

"Yes, Mister," Catherine sobbed, going for the barn in a half-run. Ellis followed her.

"Be glad to hitch up a team, Miss Conroy."

"Go on back," she said bitterly. "Go on back to your burning and killing. You mustn't miss out on—shooting—one old white-haired man!"

Ellis turned back without another word.

JEREMIAH SLIPPED forward and laid papers and straw under the front porch. In a moment it was crackling up. Jeremiah rejoined the men standing in the shadows.

"Come on out, Conroy," he yelled. "Do you want to be burned like a rat?"

Calhoun saw the sparkle and knew what was happening. His lips went tight in fury. Burning him out like a damned cheap nester!

He ran to a window and hurled a half dozen quick shots into the hackberries. None of them hit. Then, before the answering fusillade could shatter the glass, he was at the back door, taking point aim at one of the Cumberland boys.

He hit this target. He heard the yelp and chuckled in satisfaction.

So they were burning him out! Well, damn 'em, they would get a fight.

He ran back to the front. His shot hit Tolliver's horse and sent the old man spinning. Ellis Winslow ran to help his father and Calhoun dropped the son. Ellis wouldn't walk on that leg for a long time.

But Calhoun did not intend to stay there to certain death, either from shooting or burning. He dived down the kitchen steps, running with an agility that seemed impossible for a man of his years. There was a deep, wide cellar under the Conroy house, and it led up and into a greenhouse built for Myra Conroy, who hadn't seen how any woman could live without a greenhouse. The greenhouse had been abandoned these long years, with many of the glass panes broken and unreplaced.

Calhoun crawled into it, pushing his way among the earthen pots that had not been filled with fresh dirt and young plants since Myra gave up the fight against the harsh, strange ways of this new land.

He poked his head out. Off in the trees he saw a stealthy shadow, but he wisely held his fire. He crawled through the frames, tearing out the glass with his bare hands. Blood dripped from a dozen cuts but Calhoun paid them no heed.

Behind him the house was bursting into full flame. It would burn like soaked pine.

The barns were also afire and riderless horses were galloping about. Bursts of crimson lit part of the yard until it was as light as day. A dozen times Calhoun had a clear shot at one or more of the raiders. Once he could have leveled Jeremiah Gilbert, and that was a temptation hard to thrust aside.

But first he had to work his way clear. He

crawled on his belly, pushing his gun in front of him. Fifty yards, a hundred.

Finally, he pulled up in the summerhouse that had also been Myra's inspiration. She had planted roses there, and wisteria. But nothing had flourished but tie-vines. In her lifetime, and until recent years, they had cut these away each spring. Now Calhoun was grateful for them. He slipped through the palings and had cover at last.

He hesitated. The burning house threw its light over a full acre of ground, spitting fire high and far. He could lie here and wait for his shots and—

But they would get him in the end. Better to get away, to find Carter Slade, to come back and settle this score as he had settled all others in his lifetime, harshly and completely.

He hung there a moment and watched, making sure that he knew just who had dared to attack the Crown.

The Winslows, Cumberlands, Merricks, Picketts, McGees and, of course, Jeremiah!

He would remember them all.

Then, with a final smothered curse, he started running through the mesquite and canebrake. High up on the rim he could see the campfires of the Crown riders, spread out over a wide area in their hunt for Ed Kane.

He shook his fist at the mocking stars. God damn 'em, they had failed. Now they would see what Calhoun Conroy would do in revenge.

• • •

BEHIND HIM the flames rose higher. Jeremiah called his men back and they took account of the damage. Tolliver Winslow had hurt his back when his wounded horse leaped from under him. Ellis Winslow had a bad leg—Calhoun's bullet had torn through the fleshy portion, leaving an ugly, painful wound. Jim Cumberland had a shattered wrist.

The Mister had put three of them out of action.

"Anybody see old Calhoun?" Jeremiah asked anxiously.

Nobody had. It didn't make sense that the Mister would prefer to burn to death rather than take his chances in an open fight. He must have gotten away, yet no man there could understand how that was possible.

Because of the hay inside the barn burned quicker than the house. Within an hour they could approach close to the mass of burning embers. And there was light to study the ground outside.

It was Sam McGee who found Calhoun's trail. This man had trapped coyotes and coons. He could see where Calhoun had crawled through the slanting shallow roof of the greenhouse and across the open to the vine-covered summerhouse, and then had gone weaving and tottering toward the hills. McGee saw the spots of blood and chortled triumphantly.

"Here he went, men. And we winged him."

He fingered his buffalo gun. Already the McGees

had covered themselves with glory—with Jerry shooting it out with Jeff Conroy and killing his man. But Sam wasn't satisfied. He would like to be the one to bring down Calhoun Conroy.

Jeremiah grunted in satisfaction. "On foot and hit. He won't get far."

Tolliver and Ellis went riding off home. Jim Cumberland stayed in spite of his wrist. There were eight of them on Calhoun's trail, spreading out over the dark slopes, working back and forth. Jerry McGee wasn't among them. But, since they had found Jeff Conroy dead at Jerry's feet, they didn't speculate on the bartender's absence. They didn't know that Jerry, a hundred yards away in the dark, was lying on his stomach and vomiting up his insides in a long retching sickness.

Calhoun heard them. He tried to run but his legs wouldn't stand it. Already he had come several miles, and the exertion was too much for him. Three years ago his doctor had ordered him off horseback and Calhoun had yielded more obedience than he had ever given anyone, riding only to and from town, leaving supervision of the ranch to his sons and Carter Slade—mostly Carter.

He rolled into a wash, gripping his gun tightly. A fire burned within him that wasn't all fury and resentment.

The horses swept past him, one so close that Calhoun could have dropped it with a pistol shot. He did aim his gun. Then darkness swept over him.

He couldn't see and the gun dropped from his hand.

Jeremiah pulled up several miles from the still-smoldering house.

"He couldn't have come this far," he said in disgust. "We'll turn back."

Again they passed near Calhoun's hiding place.

Sam McGee stopped their floundering through the brush.

"This ain't no way to trail a man," he said in disgust. "Anybody got a lantern?"

Keith Cumberland produced one. Sam lit it and, nose close to the ground, started following the blood spots from the summerhouse.

It was easy trailing. Calhoun, heavy-footed and rolling in his run, had left a clear trail, even without the occasional dark smudges.

And he had not run far. They found him within a half hour after abandoning their horses and taking up the trail as if the Mister was a beast of the wild.

They found him half hidden by a heavy sage brush. His gun was still held tightly in his hand. Sam, seeing no more than a yard ahead of him, almost stepped on his bare swollen feet. With a yell of rage McGee threw up his buffalo gun.

But he held his fire.

Calhoun Conroy, the Mister, was already dead.

CATHERINE SADDLED her own horse, hot tears streaming down her cheeks. In this moment she was a Conroy, the daughter of white-haired, stern-lipped Calhoun, quick and long to hate, bitter in her feelings. In that moment she did not consider that what Jeremiah Gilbert and the upper valley men were doing, her father's crew had done before, many times. In that moment she forgot that she had hidden in the dark and watched Carter Slade, only three nights before, burn down another man's house and barn and pour shots into his house, hoping to strike a mark. In that moment she did not consider that this was only one burning against the Conroys, where the Crown had many in its record—that Sam McGee had lost a baby in the unfriendly night breeze when her own father had leveled his cabin by simply roping the eaves and pulling it over.

In that moment she could not admit that, at long last, Calhoun's chickens had come home to roost.

She spurred her horse down the rim road and across the Frio. She did not know that behind her Jefferson had fallen before Jerry's frantic, aimless shooting. She thought that Jefferson even now was streaking up the rim to find Carter Slade and to bring back swift retribution. She rode to Davis' to get his help. The Mister had ordered him away and she had envied Davis that freedom. But in this moment all the Conroys belonged at the Mister's side.

Davis was up from his bunk, gun in hand, at the sound of her horse. Kane also stirred. His fever had gone and he had picked up strength in these two days. Between him and the youngest Conroy had been a restrained politeness. Davis had fed him and tended to his wants without ever revealing what was in his heart—a raging jealousy and a baffled fury.

He had no hatred of Kane personally, or even jealousy. He knew full well why Mary McGee was going to marry the gray-eyed man instead of him. A union with the Crown was impossible, even with a disinherited son. There was too much bitterness for that. She had watched through long night hours over Tommy's dead body. She, too, could recall the night Calhoun had personally pulled down their cabin, and the death of a McGee baby in the chill. For long years there had been no family pride among the McGees, no hatred or resentment for what they had suffered.

But, of a sudden, Sam McGee had thrown back his shaggy head and taken to the hills with his buffalo gun. Jerry McGee had gone into battle trembling in fright and cursing himself for being a damned fool. Mary McGee, accepting a man's queer offer of marriage where a month ago she would have thrown it right back into his face, was curt and final in her dismissal of the Mister's son. She could not look him in the eye and deny her love, but she could tell him quietly and finally that their affair was at an end.

"What in the hell!" Davis gasped as Catherine burst into the clearing.

"They're burning the Crown," she sobbed, running into his arms. "And Carter is gone with the men."

"Who?"

"Jeremiah Gilbert. The Winslows. The Cumberlands. Everybody. They gave me ten minutes to get out."

She pointed across the river. The flames were a shivering red mass against the dark massiveness of the rim.

"I'll be damned!" Davis growled.

It was hard to believe. For years the Crown had not been molested.

"Jeff?"

"He slipped away. Went after Carter."

"The Mister?"

"He stayed there. You mean you haven't heard the shooting?"

"Not a thing," Davis denied slowly.

Kane called out from the cabin. "What's up?"

"They're burning us out," Davis said curtly. "All your friends, Kane."

"The McGees were there," Catherine told him cruelly. "Sam McGee had an old buffalo gun. And Jeremiah sneered. I hate that man, Davis. He has brought all this upon us. I could kill him with my bare hands."

Inside the cabin Kane slipped into his trousers. He put weight on his leg gingerly. It was stiff, but the pain was slight. He limped outside.

"Who's burning the Crown?"

"Gilbert and the upper valley men. The Winslows and the Cumberlands. And Sam McGee."

He looked toward the blaze and nodded. "I can't say I'm sorry."

"No, I guess not," Davis snapped.

"Why should he be?" demanded Catherine, suddenly remembering the fire she had looked down upon from the dark slopes.

"Well, it's done," Davis shrugged.

"Now what?" the girl demanded of her brother.

"I'll pick up where they left off," he said gently. "The Mister ran me off, but I'm still his son."

Kane caught his shoulder. "Listen, son, I—"

Davis shrugged off his hand. "I was sorry you were burned out, Kane. I still am. But if this is a war, I'm in it. Up to my neck."

"Look, friend," Kane appealed. "I've lost my house and most of my horses. Your family did it. This father of yours ordered it. His foreman brought men to my place in the dark and started shooting at everything they saw. I didn't like that either."

"Can't say I blame you. Some of us didn't like it either. That's why I helped get you out."

"But a war like that can go on and on," Kane reasoned. "I'm not trying to tell you you have to take this lying down. But, son, don't go riding off half-cocked, shooting at everybody you see. Maybe you'll get some of 'em. You won't get 'em all. There will be somebody left to get you. Feuds go on like that."

Davis' face didn't relax. "That sounds good, Kane," he admitted, something like a sneer in his voice. "But it won't work out. Even if I wanted to, they wouldn't let me stay out of it."

"Something has to work out. For twenty years the valley has been like this. I came back here looking for peace and I got into a storm. If you just have to kill somebody, if you can't sleep until you've emptied your gun, get the man who is back of it. The two men."

"Who?"

"Gilbert. Slade."

"Gilbert, yes," breathed Davis. "But Slade? He's our man."

"Slade is nobody's man but his own."

"Prove it," Davis challenged.

He was in that kind of mood. The blood of Calhoun Conroy was making his lean face ever darker.

"There's a trail over the rim. Cattle have been driven up it. Slade and Gilbert were working together."

"Impossible!"

"It's fact. Why should I lie to you, son?"

That puzzled Davis. Why indeed? Kane's glance roved to Catherine. "I've got my kick against the Crown. I'm not making a play. The valley has evened up with your breed. Let it stay there. Get rid of Gilbert. Then Carter. Let's live here—and let live."

"It can't be done."

"Why can't it? What else is there? Sling lead all over these slopes and you'll either be under the sod or you'll have to start riding. Do you want to do that?"

"I don't intend to stay and—"

"I can tell you something about that riding," Kane broke in. "All you've got when you top the far ridge is what you brought with you. And to cover any ground at all, you've got to travel light."

Davis stared at Kane a moment. He wanted to listen to this man. But the heritage of a Conroy wasn't listening. It was violence. Davis went into the cabin and pulled on his shirt. His gun belt was around his waist when he came back out.

"I'll see you, Kane," he said shortly.

"I take it you're going your own way?"

"Yes."

"What about your sister here? Where does that leave her?"

"That is hardly your worry, Mister Kane," Catherine snapped. "I hope you kill a dozen men, Davis. Shoot every man you see on sight."

Ed Kane sighed. Three nights before she had lain in his arms and accepted his kiss. But now she was her father's daughter.

"I was young once," he said wearily. "I was young and full of vinegar. This country took my mother. And my dad. It's a lonely feeling, son. Sometimes it's been so lonely that I couldn't stand it. That's what stopped me from shooting. Every time I shot I made another person lonely."

"So long, Kane," Davis said curtly, mounting his horse.

"Wait, Davis!" Catherine called. "Wait for me."

She was in the saddle as quick and nimble as any man. "I'll go with you," she told her brother.

She looked down at Kane. "Davis is right, Ed," she said gently. "There isn't anything else. If everybody in this valley could see things your way—or we could— But we Conroys are just as bad as everybody else. And everybody else is just as bad as the Conroys."

"I know that," he agreed.

Davis touched spurs and his horse went galloping away. Catherine wanted to speak to Kane again but words were slow coming to her lips. Finally, with a toss of her head, in silence she rode after her brother.

Ed Kane looked after them with a mirthless smile. He sat down, conscious suddenly of his aching leg, and rolled a cigarette. Only a red glow now showed where had stood the Mister's proud, defiant mansion. Higher up, far beyond, were the tiny glows of light that were the Crown's campfires. There wasn't, he realized with another sigh, a man in the valley who wasn't either hunting or being hunted.

All of this for what? For grass. For tempers that went white-hot. For hearts that were no less bitter because they were loyal. For slow-turning minds that soon or late thought along an ever-narrowing channel, and that didn't forget.

14

THE UNEQUAL FIGHT was over. They brought Calhoun Conroy back to his yard and he lay side by side on a blanket with Jefferson, the son he had loved and had brought up to be a replica of himself.

Now that the flush of victory was gone, they were silent before the wreckage, human and otherwise. Sam McGee, looking down at the two corpses, silently took off his hat. Jeremiah Gilbert turned away with a sneer for these men who could be raging fury one moment and soft putty the next. How easy they were to manipulate—like puppets on a string! He looked toward the specks of light on the rimtop and chortled to himself. How smoothly it had gone off! The Crown riders tomorrow would discover the fire and ride back to find the barns and bunkhouse gone, the Crown remuda scattered over the ranges, the Crown boss dead in his own front yard.

Carter could take up the reins. Who else? Gilbert

money would rebuild the barns and the corrals and replenish the remuda.

"Might as well mosey along," said Dale Merrick, suddenly ashamed for his part in the night's work. Actually the Crown had never molested his outfit. He had ridden against it because he was sick of Conroy superiority in the valley, because he resented their high-handedness and their overbearing ways. He was suddenly itching to get home, and to himself.

They rode slowly down the rim road, their horses making a loud clattering in the early morning. Davis Conroy heard them and pulled his horse back into the willows along the river. Catherine hid by his side. Davis pulled his gun but held his fire.

He was suddenly a cunning, ruthless man. Kane had warned him that one shot would bring on a fusillade in return. He had no intention of riding into 'em and leveling down on all parties. Gilbert would be first. He would pick them off one by one.

He watched them breast the first ridge on the opposite side of the river, dark quivering shapes against the pale horizon. Then, with an oath, he sent his horse galloping along the river bed, heedless of the rocks that rolled under his mount's feet but which, by some miracle, did not send him sprawling. Behind him came Catherine, her kerchief around her neck against the chill breeze. She had no idea why she was following. But there was nowhere else to go.

Davis knew where he was riding. He dipped up the creek that flowed out of Kane's timber. Behind him and above him, leisurely following the main trail, came the night riders, falling out one by one—the Cumberlands here, the Merricks at the next trail. Now Sam McGee.

Soon Gilbert would be riding along alone—toward his small, poor ranch at the extreme upper end of the valley. Davis reached the draw that divided Jeremiah's range from the Winslow grass.

"Wait here," he ordered Catherine.

She obeyed, dismounting and settling into a quivering shape under a spread of willows.

Davis rode on alone. He turned into the timber and went galloping through it. The dark shape below him was Jeremiah's cabin. He waited until he heard the banker's horse on the main trail. Then he spurred his horse to Gilbert's gate.

He was there, a motionless patch of black, when Jeremiah came up.

"Whoa!" Gilbert shouted to his horse as he saw the man at his gate. He was near-sighted, Jeremiah. He strained his eyes.

"Who is it?" he croaked, fumbling for his gun.

That was his last speech. He felt the impact before he heard the roaring. The gun he was groping for never left its holster. Jeremiah weaved in the saddle, then pitched slowly forward. One foot caught in the stirrup, and held.

His panicky horse broke back up the trail, away

from this flashing noise which had exploded right in its nostrils. Jeremiah's body hung precariously, but never wrenched itself free.

The noise behind the frightened horse spurred it to even greater speed. Jeremiah's head was a bloody shapeless thing when the pony finally slowed to a walk, and its bridle was gripped by Hugh Merrick who had heard the shots and the galloping hoofs.

"By God!" exclaimed Hugh. "It's Jeremiah."

He pulled the banker's foot free of the stirrup, laid the corpse gently across the saddle and led the still frightened but unprotesting horse to Tolliver's front gate. Sleep had not come to Tolliver, still aching from his fall. The women were up and stirring. They saw the strange gory sight at the front gate and Tolliver rolled out, holding his injured shoulder low.

"Who did it?" he demanded.

Merrick shook his head. He could guess.

"We shoulda got the other Conroy while we were about it," swore Tolliver.

He called his sons and they came out, rubbing their eyes. It still lacked a little of dawn, but there were patches where a man could see.

"We'll finish this job while we're at it," Tolliver said grimly. "In broad daylight. Get the Cumberlands. And Old Sam."

"One of the Crown riders could have doubled back," mused Merrick.

He and Tolliver looked down at Jeremiah's battered body with mingled thoughts. He was one of their own and they hated his killing. They would settle for it. But both were glad to be free of the banker's tyranny. Both were honest men, but no man is completely unselfish. Both were thinking that, to their best knowledge, Jeremiah didn't have an heir. They had bought stock in his bank long ago—when he had come to the valley it had been as a near-penniless man, pleading with them to set him up in the business all needed, and that would profit them in the long years ahead. Perhaps the mortgage against their ranches could be wiped out. There was no question of payment—they were in too deep for that. This shrewd, unscrupulous little man had gathered them all within his tentacles, and only death had set them free. If that.

Neither of them spoke such thoughts. But it struck them as a strange twist of fate that they had to go riding to avenge a killing that each, in his deep secret heart, considered a blessing. Other valley men would feel that way.

Matt Cumberland, riding up with his sons, looked at the dead man and for a moment couldn't trust himself to say a word. Nor could Sam McGee, bristling in the sudden courage and leadership that had transformed him almost in the twinkling of an eye from a beaten, cowed man into a leader.

McGee took the lead now. They followed the

trail of the frightened fugitive horse back to Jeremiah's ranch. That was easy—the blood stains, and worse, on the rocky road. There, before Jeremiah's own front gate, he had been shot down.

Not in the back, but without firing a shot in return. There wasn't an empty cylinder in his gun.

McGee bent over and studied the trail of the other horse. Now daylight was breaking over the valley. This was the second time this pale, chilled morning he had followed a man's trail. Now he needed no lantern. He walked a few paces, then climbed back on his horse. He could follow this one from the saddle.

For it led back to the river bed, and there rocks had been overturned in Davis' gallop, which were plainer evidence than tracks. Here two horses had stood, and finally had turned off.

Davis and Catherine had, after a moment's indecision, turned up the rim to join the Crown riders, to call them back off Ed Kane's trail.

Across the river, outlined a moment against the slopes, they saw Davis and Catherine.

They had ridden slow to rest Davis' horse. They heard the shouts behind them, and turned to see a dozen men on their trail, and to hear the booming roar of Sam McGee's buffalo gun warning them to stop.

Both dug in their spurs. But Davis' pony was winded. The first steep slope found it faltering under him.

"Go get—Slade," Davis panted. "I'll—hold 'em off."

Catherine bent low over her horse's mane and fairly flew up the ridges. This was a blooded mount—Calhoun boasted that his remuda had pure Kentucky strain. And this girl could ride.

Behind her Davis pulled and waited. He did not fall into an ambush and start firing. The odds against him were too great. He would have to stall, and to hope Carter Slade came in time.

Tolliver Winslow lowered his rifle from a dead bead when he saw that Davis was quietly sitting his horse.

"Wants to give up," he growled.

Quickly they surrounded the youngest Conroy, who never budged from his horse.

"Yes, gentlemen?" Davis asked crisply.

"We figgered you would fight," grumbled Tolliver. "What do you expect to get by giving up?"

"What would I get by fighting?" shrugged Davis. "I have done you men no harm."

Indecision split their ranks. Had he shot back and taken to the brush, they all would have pressed on his trail, quick to utilize any chance to shoot him down. But here he stood, seemingly unafraid and defiant, with no motion toward the gun at his belt. They were stumped. This wasn't in the cards. When you rode to wipe out an outfit, that outfit was supposed to fight back.

"We took Crown bullying long enough, Conroy," snapped Tolliver. "We don't take it no more."

Inside Davis was boiling but he smiled coldly and craftily.

"My outfit is below the Crown across the river," he said lightly. "My father chased me off three days ago. The split was *bueno* by me. I own no part of the Crown and don't want any."

They were afraid he was stalling. They could look high up and see Catherine's chestnut flitting from slope to slope, climbing higher and higher to where the early morning campfires gleamed on the upper rim, to where Carter Slade rode with Crown men like Peck Purdy. Each man in his heart had already thought about what would happen when Slade and those lean drifters came down out of the hills and found the Crown burned and Calhoun lying dead on a blanket near the ruins. It was not a pleasant thought. It would take all of them to give the Crown anywhere near an even battle, and they would be facing men who could outride them and outshoot them.

Yet this had been started. It had to be finished.

Tolliver cleared his throat. "Somebody shot Jeremiah Gilbert. Right at his gate. Didn't even give him a chance to draw."

"I'm glad to hear it," Davis said politely, and coldly. He had Calhoun's coldness at this moment without the Mister's flaming temper. "My congratulations to the man—if you find him. And the drinks are on me."

Matt Cumberland's growl was echoed by every man present. "Enough of that talk, Conroy," Matt said sternly. "We followed your trail from Gilbert's. We figger you're the guilty man."

Davis shrugged his shoulders. "Ride to town and swear out a warrant. I don't mind standing trial."

For a moment there was no answer. Then came Tolliver's voice, low and grim.

"You're standing trial out here—this morning. And if you're guilty, you'll swing from a hackberry limb."

Davis paled. He had not expected this.

Tolliver turned to Sam. "McGee, you've followed his trail. Is this the man who killed Jeremiah?"

"His horse was outside Gilbert's gate," Sam said slowly, fully aware of what his testimony meant. Then, hesitantly: "We oughta be sure, Mister Winslow. Suppose we double back real slow-like."

Tolliver nodded.

Matt Cumberland reached for Davis' gun. Conroy offered no protest. He permitted his horse to be led with that same cold smile still on his lips.

Once he glanced back over one shoulder. Catherine's chestnut wasn't in sight. Perhaps she had reached a Crown campfire and Crown riders were already on their way to his rescue.

Perhaps they could get there. Sam McGee was taking his time on the trail. He lifted each leg of Davis' horse and showed every man interested the shoe marks. A nail missing on the right shoe. See? Here were the same tracks.

Each time Sam was rewarded with silent, patient nods. No man present liked what was before him. A running fight was all right. A hanging was something else.

They clattered back to Jeremiah's gate. The banker's broken corpse lay on the front porch, covered with a saddle blanket. Here, at the gate, were the conclusive tracks.

Tolliver dismounted to examine them, as did Matt Cumberland. The two stiff, white-haired men, whose brawny sons waited quietly for their verdict, exchanged comments and glances. Unquestionably here was the print of a horse missing a nail in its right shoe.

"I don't like to make such a statement," Sam McGee said slowly, "but I can pretty near swear this horse was at this gate not over three hours ago."

Matt Cumberland examined the cylinders of Davis' gun. It had been fired recently.

Tolliver motioned them to leave their horses. They squatted in a circle around the seventy-year-old man who had been the first to graze a cow in this valley.

"Gentlemen," Tolliver said softly, "you see the

picture. Davis Conroy, whether he wants to own up to it or not, waited here at this gate and shot down Jeremiah Gilbert without giving him a chance to fight back. It was murder, cold-blooded murder. I figger there is just one way to treat a murderer."

"What was it when you attacked the Crown last night?" demanded Davis. "Was that murder?"

"It was the same thing as the Crown attacking Kane," Tolliver answered sternly. "It was fighting fire with fire. Conroy, you got no call to mouth. There's been damned little lead thrown in this valley that the Crown didn't sling. Every man here has lost his own blood kin fighting your people. Most of the time the odds were heavy on your side. None of us ever brought in paid gun-slicks to do our killing for us."

Davis looked away—again toward the high, frowning rim. There was no point in telling these grim determined men that he had never approved of his father's way of running a ranch, or of making war. Nothing he could say would alter their opinions, or their decision.

When he didn't answer, Tolliver's glance moved clockwise, from owlish Sam McGee to hard-bitten Matthew Cumberland.

"What do you say, boys?" Tolliver asked.

Nobody answered. Finally Matt stood up.

"I'll get a rope," he said curtly. "Jeremiah ought to have one around somewhere."

• • •

KANE GAVE UP trying to sleep. Faint sounds of shooting had drifted to him all evening. His fever was down and his leg would take his weight, though with some pain. He pulled on his clothes and saddled one of Davis' horses and rode toward the shooting.

It was almost dawn. By the time he crossed the rim road it was light, and he could see Catherine and Davis ahead of him, then the pursuit behind. He saw Catherine riding ahead alone and Davis standing to face the accusations of Matthew Cumberland and Tolliver Winslow. He was higher than all of this. He was midway up the rim and the stirring Crown riders might have looked down and seen him.

Catherine did see him as she crossed the narrow Blue Creek and cut over toward the main road. He signaled to her, and was grateful when she turned her horse in his direction.

She explained tersely. He listened gravely, then nodded.

"But don't go after Slade," he said. "I'll help Davis."

She hesitated, unwilling to trust him. "Carter can bring the boys and wipe this valley out," she said coldly. "One Peck Purdy is worth a half dozen Cumberlands."

"I doubt that," he snapped. "Besides, some of your men are teaming up with rustlers."

She paled. "I dare you to prove it!" she challenged.

"I can."

He caught her arm. "Look, Catherine," he said wearily, "I ask you to trust me. I'm sick of killing. Those men won't harm Davis, I'll promise you that. Now you ride back to the line cabin and wait there. I'll send Davis right along."

"What are you going to do?" she asked.

"There's a gent waiting for me on top of the rim," he said grimly. "I'm going to stop them from stringing up Davis, then get that gent down here to tell his story. I figger when he gets through we'll know who to go after. And it won't be Davis."

"Carter?"

Kane shrugged his shoulders. "I guessed that before. You doubted me. It's the other gent's story anyhow. I'll let him tell it."

She searched his face, and was satisfied with what she saw.

Kane rode after the valley men. Twice he shouted in the hope of attracting their attention, but they didn't hear him. A rope noose was already around Davis' neck when finally they saw him, and waited for him to gallop up.

"Aren't you boys rushing things?" he asked calmly.

"This man killed Jeremiah Gilbert," snapped Tolliver.

He turned to Davis, whose dark face was pale but

whose eyes were unwavering. “I did kill Gilbert,” Conroy admitted. “Right here.”

Ed rolled a cigarette. “Let’s talk this over,” he suggested.

There were impatient growls, but no resistance. No man except Ed Kane could have stopped their lynching. They would have fought off a sheriff or even a Ranger. And Ed couldn’t have stopped it, except in the way he did—with unhurried casualness.

“I think maybe we’ve had enough of this killing,” he said, looking around with sharp, appraising eyes. “We’ve had worse than a feud in this valley—we’ve had rustlers picking off our profits. I stumbled onto their trail a while back. I followed them over the rim. Up there in a cabin fixed up secure with rawhide, I got one of ’em who is willing to talk—in return for a fresh horse and a running start. I told him I thought you boys would be interested.”

“Later,” growled Matthew Cumberland. “Right now we’re finishing up with the Conroys.”

“Reckon you’re getting off the main trail,” Kane drawled. “So Davis shot down Jeremiah Gilbert. Didn’t he have a right to? What about his folks?”

“Gilbert didn’t kill ’em.”

“He didn’t know that,” shrugged Ed. “Wouldn’t have made any difference if he had. Gilbert has kept this valley steamed up against the Crown. Davis was smart enough to know that.”

"Murder is murder," said Tolliver. "Let us alone, Kane."

"Reckon I can't, Tolliver. I'm tired of this burning and shooting and I'm taking a hand. I tell you I can show you who was running stock out of this valley. I'll bring that man down here and let him tell his story. It'll shock you some. Mebbe, when he gets through, you won't be in such an all-fired hurry to string up another Conroy."

This speech brought a flurry of indecision. Finally Tolliver Winslow settled it.

"Get your man," he snapped. "We'll listen."

Ed looked down at his injured leg. "I'm not much of a hand at riding right now," he said mildly. "How about sending one of your boys, Tolliver?"

It was a Cumberland who finally went. They settled in the shade and smoked and waited. Tolliver came over to argue with Kane.

"Might as well get it over with now—all of it," argued the old man. "The Crown has made trouble around here a long time."

"Davis ain't the Crown," Ed pointed out. "Old Calhoun disowned him. Gave him the lower canebrake pasture and just what stock was in it."

"He took up Calhoun's fight," countered Tolliver.

"Wouldn't any son do that?" Ed demanded. "Do you think any less of him for that?"

"No," Tolliver reluctantly admitted.

It was three hours before Keith Cumberland returned with Black Ben. The rustler's muscles were so stiff from lack of circulation that he could hardly stay in the saddle. Keith had tied him into the stirrups.

"Friend, you played a dirty trick on me," Black Ben complained to Kane. "Leaving a man tied up like that for this long."

"I was interrupted," Kane said dryly.

Black Ben looked around him, still unafraid. "These the gents I got to talk to?"

Ed nodded.

Black Ben licked his lips.

"Gents, Kane here made a proposition. He got the goods on me running cattle out of this valley."

There were growls and Matthew Cumberland reached for his rifle. Black Ben grinned.

"Not too many cattle," he said cheerfully. "Just enough to get by. Me, I'm just a hired hand. For a fresh horse and chance to run, I'm willing to tell who in this valley started me out, and who has ramrodded the whole business."

"You mean a ranchman—one of us?" demanded Tolliver.

"Sure."

"Who?" barked Cumberland.

Black Ben looked to Kane. "They ain't made me any guarantee."

"I'll make it for them," Kane promised.

"Go ahead, talk," scowled Tolliver. "We'll give you your start. Rats like you don't bother us much. We want the man with the brains."

The rustler nodded. "*Bueno.* Jeremiah Gilbert."

Not one of these grim silent men stirred. If they were surprised, they didn't show it.

"Carter Slade," added Black Ben.

Kane spoke up. "This Purdy. Was he in on it?"

"Not as I know of," Black Ben said instantly. "A podner of mine and I took the cattle over the rim and down to a ranch south of Encinal. Gilbert owns that one too. We just got good riding wages."

No one seemed inclined to talk. "So Gilbert is dead," Kane said harshly. "He bled this valley white. He held every man here under his thumb. It's good riddance."

Now no one challenged his statement. Kane studied them a moment, then limped over and set Davis free.

"Get going," he said gruffly. But Davis held back.

Black Ben climbed into his saddle. "I figger that goes for me too," he said with a grin. "So long, gents."

There was no protest and Black Ben was off in a run. No one seemed to notice. Every eye was on Ed Kane. In this moment of surprise and indecision, they had to have a leader.

"Conroy can go where he likes," Kane said. "The feud between the Crown and the valley is over.

Now we'll go after Slade, and we'll give him a rope like he deserves."

It hurt him to say that. Carter Slade had been his friend.

Tolliver squinted up at the horsemen who were mere specks on the rimside.

"That ain't so easy, Kane," he murmured. "The hired gun-slicks will fight with Slade."

"No, it ain't easy," Kane agreed. "But what else is there, Tolliver?"

It was Matthew Cumberland who answered. "It's something we shoulda done a long time ago."

15

KANE STUDIED their faces. He had ridden with posses, many of them. These men, though haggard from loss of sleep, from riding and fighting all night, were ready to ride and fight again. They knew what this fight would be. To the finish against the strength of the Crown, the calm, sure Peck Purdys, the grim, ruthless Carter Slades. None of them liked it. But it was onc which had to be made. And it was right and proper that Ed Kane should lead them.

He shifted his weight in the saddle, the leg still paining him when he rested his weight upon it.

"Let's go," he said curtly.

They rode in a bunch, Kane in front, Sam McGee just behind, Matt Cumberland and Tolliver

Winslow and Hugh Merrick next. Ellis Winslow, with a leg wound worse than Kane's, sat his saddle with a white, strained face. There were two of Matt Cumberland's sons and two of his riders. There were five boys from the Winslow outfit, two others from the Lazy Z besides Merrick. The numerical odds might possibly be in their favor—no one knew exactly how many men Carter had.

They splashed across the creek. "They'll know what's up if we ride all bunched up like this," frowned Tolliver.

"We want 'em to know," Kane shrugged. "This is the last fight in this valley."

They took it slow and easy. "Every man check his gun and belt," called out Kane, halfway up the rim.

That advice was unnecessary. Every man had done that long ago. And had made sure his cartridge belt was on tight and pistol flap was loose. Sam McGee was offered a Winchester but he stuck to his buffalo gun, patting its big stock fondly.

"The old gal can hold her own with these newfangled contraptions," he insisted.

Tolliver Winslow, sharper-eyed than his juniors, let out a short, small "Hey!" and pointed up the rim. They saw the Crown's riders come off the high ridge in a cloudy swirl of dust. Kane studied them a moment.

"They're heading for timber," he said. "We'll speed up."

He swept ahead at a full gallop. They clattered up the rim road, going toward the Crown outfit at a sharp angle. A coyote rose out of a dry wash and loped away. They pulled in close to thread their way through an area of scab rock behind the Crown headquarters. When they were past it, spreading out again, the Crown riders were only a mile or less away, still between them and the timber.

Now they were climbing fast and the horses were puffing. Kane let 'em blow. They couldn't beat the Crown in the race for the timber. The first pines were only five hundred yards away.

Kane recognized Slade. And Peck Purdy.

He threw his rifle to his shoulder and got Slade's bay between the sights. The range was probably too long but a shot wouldn't hurt. Dust kicked up in front of Carter's mount.

There was a booming in Kane's ears, almost bursting their drums. Sam McGee's buffalo gun was at work.

But the range was still too far. Slade and his riders dipped into the pines. For a moment they were out of sight, then Kane saw a flicker of motion.

"They're cutting toward the rim road," he shouted. "We'll cut in front of them."

They turned from west to northwest, swinging around the pines, up and down with the potholes of the uneven ground. There was no shock from this breathless pursuit, so deep was the cushioning layer of humus. Sun brightened the overhead green and the day's heat began to cut the long-held chill of early morning. Kane rode with his bad leg free of the stirrup in an effort to ease the pain which slugged its way from toe to hip. Sweat collected under his hatband. The raw bruises around his mouth began to throb and burn. Tolliver stayed with him. This white-haired man was still a great rider, still a physical giant among men.

Strangely enough, Sam McGee, who had ridden little in recent years, was the third man as the line spread out, as one horse began to outdistance another. Sam rode like an Indian, his shoulders going high at each jump of the horse, his feet pushed straight and his arms carrying the gun up against his chest. He shot first when the Crown riders came up through the deeper timber, also riding fast. At his blast the Crown group scattered. At once both outfits were wheeling around the gray and golden light.

Here among the thin pines the fight was on.

Kane saw Slade as the latter threw his horse behind the partial shelter of a pine. Men on horseback would find uncertain cover, but also men on horseback would be uncertain shots. Ed rushed the tree, rifle to his shoulder. The sound of this quick explosion was compressed beneath the pine boughs, rolling through the corridors of the hills, slamming and echoing and breaking into smaller whorls of sound in the deep distance.

The tumult was heard at every house in the valley and all knew instantly what it was. And all, even those women who sobbed and went red-eyed about their household tasks, stopping again and again to gaze upward at the shaggy rim, as if there was something about its stern face that would tell them what they wanted to know, breathed a sigh of relief. There could be no other way. For years they had hoped for and sought another way. This would have been the easiest from a long way back.

A bullet chipped the edge of a tree, shedding bark particles on Kane's hat as he rushed forward. Slade fired and faded. Kane's shots went wide as his pony bucked.

The alternate patches of sunlight and shadow blurred a man's eyes and the crisscrossing motion of the riders made them hard to place. Kane swung wider, hoping to outrun Slade. A Crown rider came into the open, shooting from his saddle. He snapped at Kane. Ed, sensing the danger, threw himself low in the saddle.

The terrific boom shook him and his horse. It came from behind him, and from one side. He saw the Crown rider pitch from the saddle. It was a direct hit.

He turned without slowing his horse. Sam McGee gave a wild yell that screeched out above the din of galloping horses and roaring guns. There was a light in his eyes that caused Kane to grin.

Another Crown man gave him a target. As the valley men were after Slade, so the Crown men were pressing toward Kane. Again McGee's buffalo gun shattered other noises into thin rattling. The Crown rider sailed through the air, his horse pitching crazily, and finally falling behind him.

Both outfits were riding in a circle, coming closer and closer. They kept wheeling and swinging, the slopes shattered by the close-held detonations, dust thickening and the smell of powder rank in the air. Through this heavy evil haze Kane sighted Slade again. Despite the danger of such rashness, he spurred his horse directly forward. There was lightning in his face, crashing thunder in his ears. But the Crown rider who broke out of the brush just in front of him missed at such point-blank range. Now he was breaking for cover, and he didn't make it.

Again Ed turned. Tolliver Winslow this time. Ed spurred ahead with another grin. Old men could hold their own in range wars. Somehow fury, long stored up, could atone for faded youth.

Slade bobbed up ahead, a flickering elusive shape in the timber. Kane bore for him. Now Carter came in full view, head on. Kane had a shot but his horse rolled under him and it didn't land. Then Slade faded behind the close-ranked trees once more and Kane saw the rump of the Crown foreman's horse appear and disappear.

Dust clung to the air and where sunlight slid through the overhead branches this dust boiled into stained-gold brilliance. The roaring around Kane was faster pitched. Through it came the sound of McGee's buffalo gun with swelling crescendo.

He heard Tolliver's hoarse shout: "By God, they're running. After 'em, boys."

And then a crashing, and Tolliver's loud cursing.

It was true—some of the Crown men were in flight. Down the rim now, heads low over their horses' manes. Crashing right through the wild-eyed valley men who were shooting from pitching, reeling horses. One man dropped.

But Kane saw with a swift glance that the fight was not over yet, that ahead of him were still a handful of Crown riders, that Peck Purdy, taller than ever among these straight pines, was now riding with Carter Slade. There were two others, four of them in all, breaking through the trees ahead, plunging out of them and up a steep grade, across a rocky arroyo and now up the twisting gullies of the mid-rim.

Ed stopped to let his horse blow. No use to carry on a chase with weary ponies. Tolliver rode up, holding one arm. He was on a Crown horse—his own had gotten away. Blood soaked his shirt and powder stained his bushy white eyebrows and thick matted white hair until he was an eerie sight.

"God damn 'em, let's finish it," he roared. "We'll run Slade and Purdy down."

Kane shook his head and calmly rolled a cigarette. "It's a long trail," he said. "We'll need fresh horses."

Now the other warriors gathered around. The Crown men who had fled into the valley could go unchallenged. They were drifting men who had been chased off ranges before. When their foreman broke into flight, they felt all loyalty past, all restrictions gone. The Crown that had hired them was whipped and broken. Theirs was an impersonal feud. They would ride on to another range, and probably take up again with a different outfit the ceaseless bloody war for grass.

Kane quickly checked their casualties. Tolliver Winslow wounded. Ellis Winslow had lost his horse and had a fall which had done his leg no good. Hugh Merrick was dead. This ranchman who had less cause than any to fight the Crown was their only fatality. Sam McGee was untouched, his fire unquenched.

"Let's don't sit here all day, Kane," complained the nester. "Let's get after 'em."

Again Kane shook off their impatience. He continued to study his men. The Cumberland boys, two Winslows, one of Merrick's riders—he stabbed at them with a finger.

"You boys ride with me."

To Winslow he said: "We want fresh horses. Meet us across the rim. Take the Uvalde road."

Now they saw the wisdom of his strategy. They

could not ride down the Crown stragglers with tired horses. But they could keep on their trail until fresh horses came, keep prodding them. And, of course, they would be ready for a fight anytime Slade wanted it.

All were satisfied but McGee. The nester rushed forward.

"I reckon you overlooked me, Mister Kane," he said boldly. "I figger on being in at the finish."

"Sure, Sam," Kane smiled. "Bring old Bertha along. We can use her—and you."

The fleeing Slade and his three companions were now small specks on the steepening rim. Kane and his riders started in pursuit at a leisurely lope.

No call to hurry. Stay out of rifle range. But keep 'em moving.

This was an old story to Ed Kane. He had learned such patience the hard way. He could be calm and casual like this. One manhunt was just like another.

THE PURSUIT DRAGGED. Ahead, Carter Slade and his three Crown henchmen slowed their horses into a lope, and then a walk. Behind, Ed Kane and his posse rode as slowly.

An hour, two hours. They crossed over the rim road and toward the wastelands. Anywhere along here Slade could make a fight, using nature's ambush. But he didn't.

Lagging farther behind, Kane waited for fresh

horses. And men. They came galloping up, the Winslow boys pulling a dozen riderless mounts. And there was the Merrick outfit in full force, each with an extra horse. Eight fresh men and a dozen ponies.

Ed dismounted and drew a crude map in the dust. He addressed his talk to Matthew Cumberland.

"They're riding slow. Cut below 'em and come up Rattlesnake Canyon to this little Spick town. You might beat 'em there. Take six men with you and try it."

Matthew nodded. "We'll keep on their trail," Kane said grimly.

Cumberland picked his men. The Merrick riders. One of his own sons. At Kane's suggestion they carried the extra horses. They had to ride fast. Kane and his men could keep going on their same mounts. The Crown ponies were just as tired.

Matthew galloped off, five men behind him. They disappeared into the flats and were seen a moment later racing down the canyon. It deepened ahead. A mile farther up and there would have been no crossing.

They kept riding, rifles ready in their hands. Now Carter Slade and his three hirelings were out of sight. But their trail was fresh. They were traveling faster.

Kane put himself in Slade's place. Horses weary under them. Odds hopelessly against them. They would hope for fresh horses at Encinal. Given new mounts they would have only sixty miles or so in a bee-line for the border, and they could make it. Kane was deliberately letting them nurse that hope.

Now the ground dropped no longer. It was level country. Ranch country. Here was grass in wet weather but uncertain water. Outfits came up from south of Encinal and the Webb County hills to use this grass. It had been dry a long time and they saw no cattle. Here the timber was sparse and ragged.

Ahead, Carter Slade was satisfied with the way he was leaving his pursuit behind. Their horses would not take a sustained run. They galloped a while, then let their mounts blow. But, mounting a high ridge, they saw the valley men several miles behind them.

At Encinal, Slade climbed from his horse in front of a combination saloon-restaurant. Here were Mexicans, sullen and frightened before these four Americans.

Slade searched his vocabulary. *"Dinero? Mustangs? Pronto?"*

His answer was a *"no sabe Americano."*

But there were two horses hitched to the rail. Slade nodded to Purdy and they strode inside. Two vaqueros were drinking tequila. Slade waved a gun in their faces and gruffly announced they were trading horses.

Before he could impress upon their startled minds that it was no robbery, but a trade, galloping hoofs shook the tiny frame building. Outside there was a cry of alarm, then a rattle of gunfire.

Slade leaped to the window. Matthew Cumberland and his men had reached the town. Slade cursed and slung a quick shot.

Then he ducked past the bar and out of the back door. Peck Purdy was ahead of him.

Outside, the two Crown riders dropped their guns. One of Hugh Merrick's riders was dead, and Cumberland was swearing at Slade's henchmen.

"You cooked your goose," growled Matt. "We wouldn't have strung you up if it hadn't been for that."

Behind the saloon, Slade took stock of the little Mexican town. Only a handful of houses—these of the one-room variety. He pushed into an abandoned barn. Matthew Cumberland came around the corner of the saloon and Carter ducked low.

Cumberland could speak the Mexican lingo. He called the saloon keeper and the two vaqueros and told them what would happen if they didn't reveal the hiding place of the two *Americanos* who had come into the saloon. The vaqueros shrugged their shoulders and murmured *"no sabe."* The guns did not throw them into a panic.

But the saloon keeper pleaded. The senor must realize they knew nothing of the *Americanos*. With a curse Cumberland spread out a dragnet. Losing reason in his anger, he ordered the buildings fired.

Mexican families poured out, pleading. Unrelenting, Cumberland set fire to their buildings himself. Two, three houses, went up in smoke.

The flames spread. Carter Slade heard them crackle and knew the barn would blaze up any moment now. He licked his lips.

He must come out fighting. He called for Purdy but there was no answer. He had no way of knowing that the lean gun-slick was even now stealing around the corner of the saloon.

Slade gripped his holster, lowered his head and rushed out. Rushed blindly, in a sudden panic. He shot at a tall man standing across from the barn, but missed. The return lead sang close to him, but he ducked around a corner of the barn.

Keith Cumberland was coming around the barn. Slade ran smack into him and the two of them went tumbling in a heap.

"I got him!" yelled Keith, recovering his wits first.

Help came quickly. In a moment Carter Slade stood unarmed and tied, his nostrils quivering in rage, his eyes wild and red. Then the fury died and in its place was a shaking fear.

"What are you gonna do with me?"

"You'll see," growled Matt.

In the confusion of trapping Slade, and fighting him down, Peck Purdy reached the corner of the saloon unchallenged. One of the Merrick riders lounged there watching the horses. Purdy brought his gun butt down in a savage slash, and the Merrick hand toppled noiselessly to the dust.

Peck threw himself into the saddle of a squealing chestnut and raked the spurs deep.

Now he was seen. Shots rained around him. His pitching horse saved him. He hung low over the animal's head and kept raking with the spurs. The chestnut leaped again, then lowered its head, took the bit in its teeth and shot off at a furious run. Purdy let it go for a mile or more, then wrenched its head up. For a moment the chestnut fought him. Horse and man had it out.

Then the pony obeyed the cruel demanding spurs and raced on.

Behind, Keith Cumberland and two other Merrick men gave chase. But Purdy, with the swift judgment of his kind, had stolen the fastest horse in the valley—Keith's favorite pony. He put miles between them. They lost his zig-zagging trail in the rocky washes below Encinal Creek.

The border was an afternoon's hard riding away. Peck Purdy could have made it.

But he turned back instead. He rested his chestnut by grass and water and killed a cottontail. Flight across the border was not for Peck Purdy—not yet! And never.

KANE SPURRED his weary horse into a lope as he saw from the crowded hitching rack that Matthew

Cumberland had already arrived and that the fight was over.

Matt and the Merrick riders, including the man who had been felled by Peck Purdy, were drinking in the saloon.

"Thought you'd take all day," Cumberland grinned at Kane. "Take a look-see out behind and see how we've amused ourselves."

Kane stepped through the back door. Swinging from a cottonwood limb were three bodies. He had seen hanged men before, but one of these was Carter Slade, and the sight sickened him. He was grateful for the drink Cumberland pressed upon him.

They waited until late afternoon for Keith Cumberland and the other Merrick riders to return.

"The —— got away," grumbled Keith as he rode up, soaked with perspiration and dust. "He got my horse. Nothing in this country can catch that horse."

16

THEY CAMPED for the night halfway back to the rim and gorged on fresh venison. Sam McGee sat proudly among them, refilling his coffee cup again and again. Men spoke to Sam respectfully, even joshing him a little because of his outmoded buffalo gun. He answered back in kind, a sparkle in his eyes they had never seen before. He had a story to illustrate every viewpoint. They roared at his stories until a late hour.

For a long time after that, valley riders dropped over to Sam's when work was off and the hours dragging.

"Let's ride over and hear some of Sam's yarns," they would say.

Clattering over the rim, they met Tolliver Winslow. He, Matthew and Ed talked a moment. They decided to meet at Tolliver's that night and discuss what would be done about the Crown and Jeremiah's place back up in the timber. Someone would speak for Hugh's widow.

They fell out, one by one, until Kane was riding alone, and the benchland with its mass of charred embers was near at hand. Ed rode slowly, his senses dulled by his thoughts and by fatigue. The leg was still stiff and pained him whenever his black pony broke out of an easy walk.

He didn't hear the gentle scraping that at any other time would have warned him instantly a horse was in the rocky shale ahead. In fact, not until Peck Purdy spoke did he realize that someone was ahead of him on the trail, was waiting there like a frozen statue.

"Make your play, Kane," Purdy said quietly.

Ed was startled. He had thought Purdy long-gone into Mexico.

But here was the lean man back in the heart of the valley where he would be shot down on sight.

"Is this necessary, Purdy?" Kane asked quietly. "You got away once. You can get away again. You got the drop on me."

Purdy shifted his weight in the saddle. "Reckon it is, Kane," he drawled. "In the first place, Slade hired me to handle you. He asked me at San Antone if I could down you in a fight. I told him I thought so."

"Slade's gone," Kane growled. He had no heart for this challenge. He knew it for what it was—a vain man's play. Gunmen everywhere were like that. Peck Purdy would flee this range, but not until he had settled the doubt in his own mind, one way or another.

"You're wasting time, Kane," Purdy said gently.

The former Ranger sighed. There was no avoiding it.

"Get off your horse," ordered the outlaw. "Start walking backward. When I shoot in the air, turn and make your play."

Ed obeyed. Five steps, six. He could hear Purdy's high heels clattering on the rocks. Then the roar—Purdy had given the signal!

He whirled. Something bit at his arm as he shot. Ed Kane had never been the fastest Ranger with a gun. Other men could outdraw him. But Kane had learned that a single shot was enough, if a man could make it so. Purdy's bullet ripped his sleeve. His shot stopped the lean outlaw from walking forward.

The gun dropped from Purdy's hand. He looked at Kane, peering forward and blinking his eyes as if the light were uncertain and vision was difficult. There was astonishment on his lean face, his mouth open.

Now his legs gave out. He swayed forward.

"By God, Kane," he whispered, "you did it."

He slipped to the ground, falling a little at a time. Finally he lay flat, looking up at his conqueror with a thin smile.

"You're some hand, Kane," he murmured. "I wish we could have—ridden the river—together."

A shudder shook his long lanky frame—and that was all.

Kane tried to pull his body over the saddle but the exertion was too much for his leg. And Keith Cumberland's chestnut had broken for home with the first gunfire. Ed covered the dead outlaw with his slicker and rode on toward the benchland.

Everything was gone—corrals, barn, house. He looked around and sighed. At least there had been a house when he had first returned. Here Davis Conroy and Mary McGee had met and loved each other in defiance of what the results of such a love could be. Ed rolled a cigarette. Then, with another sigh, he rode on to Tolliver Winslow's for the meeting. Tolliver wouldn't mind setting another place for supper.

Ellis was in bed, an infection in his leg. The tireless Winslow women hovered over him and kept fires blazing in the kitchen. Tolliver and Ed talked a moment and then, with the quick easy informality of the country, Tolliver invited Kane to help him feed the horses. They sauntered toward the corral, deep in their talk of what they could do with the Crown and Jeremiah's spread, of cross-fences and round-up pastures that could be used by them all.

They saw Davis as they started back to the house. He came riding at a gallop. He fairly flung himself from the saddle and stalked toward them, his dark face set in determined lines.

"What's this I hear about a meeting tonight?" he demanded of Kane.

"There is one—yes," Tolliver growled.

They had set this Conroy free, but Tolliver could not forgive at once. Davis glowered at them, standing with his legs far apart.

"Do you want the Crown in?" he demanded. "Do you want us to ride with you or are we still by ourselves?"

"You figger on rebuilding the Crown?" Ed asked.

"Sure," Davis snapped. "It's mine now."

"We'd like the Crown in," Kane said, speaking before Tolliver Winslow could make his answer. "We want peace in this valley, Davis. We want to live and let live."

"So do I," said the youngest Conroy.

He gave Kane an even defiant glance. “I’ll be away a spell. I’m going to San Antonio. To see about a loan to rebuild the house and barns. When I get back, I’m hiring new riders. The Crown will be here like it always was, except—”

Now he looked to Tolliver. “Except we’ll be a good neighbor,” he finished quietly.

“Good!” Tolliver approved. He held out his hand. “I like your talk, son. Call on me and mine for help in rounding up your stock. And come on in—maw can put an extra plate on the table.”

Davis hesitated, then accepted. His dark eyes still studied Kane’s face. He let Tolliver walk on ahead.

“I’m getting married, Kane,” he said curtly.

“To Mary?” Ed guessed.

“Yes. I told her I would face you with it. She didn’t want to go back on her promise. She would have stuck with it come hell or high water. But I wouldn’t take no. Anything you got to say about it—say it to me.”

Kane recalled another time Davis had bristled before him, when they had met on the rim road and he had charged Conroy with using his house to carry on an illicit affair. He smiled again, as he had smiled that time.

“My congratulations,” he murmured, holding out a hand. “You’re a lucky man.”

Davis took his hand with a sigh of relief. “Gosh, Kane,” he exclaimed, “you don’t know how much better that makes me feel. And it will tickle Mary pink."

"We'll announce it tonight," Kane said, "at the meeting. I think it will go over big with the valley men."

HE WAS REBUILDING his corral. The lumber had just been hauled out from Cotulla that afternoon and he was head over heels in the sweat and haste of digging postholes, always the dirtiest job. He didn't hear her ride up, and not until she spoke was he aware of her presence.

"Hello, Ed," she said, so close to him that he almost touched her as he turned.

She was wearing a white silk shirt that showed the swell of her bosom, that made him conscious of his sweat and griminess.

"Sit down and talk to me while I blow," he grinned, motioning to the hackberries and taking out his papers and tobacco.

"You've fixed things up some," she observed, looking around her.

"Some," he admitted. "It's hot work. I guess it'll be fall before I can start looking after my cattle right."

"I suppose so," she sighed.

"How is Davis? And Mary?"

"Fine. They're riding over to see you soon."

"How do you like your sister-in-law?"

She sensed what was behind his question. "I

think," she said slowly, "that Davis is a very lucky man."

"So do I," he nodded.

"Much luckier than you," Catherine told him. Her eyes danced with devilment and daring. She leaned forward, and the white shirt fell away from her shoulders. "You missed a bet there, Ed Kane. When you let Mary go—you just had me left."

A smile touched Ed Kane's face. "Every man has to play his own hand his own way," he said slowly.

The invitation in her eyes was too much to resist. He reached for her.

"I'll stand pat on mine," he whispered.

Curtis Bishop was born in Tennessee but lived most of his life in Texas, where he traveled with rodeos and worked for several daily newspapers as a feature writer. Much of his newspaper writing dealt with characters, landmarks, and institutions of the Old West. In 1943 he also began writing fiction for the magazine market, especially Fiction House magazines, including *Action Stories*, *North-West Romances*, and *Lariat Story Magazine*. During World War Two, Bishop served with the Latin-American and Pacific staffs of the Foreign Broadcast Intelligence Service. His first attempt at a novel was titled "Quit Texas—or Die!" in *Lariat Story Magazine* (3/46). Subsequently he expanded this story to a book-length novel titled *Sunset Rim*, published by Macmillan in 1946. "Bucko-Sixes—Wyoming Bound!", which appeared in *Lariat Story Magazine* (7/46), was expanded to form *By Way Of Wyoming*, also published in 1946 by Macmillan. These were followed by *Shadow Range* (Macmillan, 1947), an expansion of "Hides for the Hang-Tree Breed" in *Lariat Story Magazine* (11/46). Although Bishop continued to write for the magazine market for the rest of the decade, his next novel didn't appear until 1950 when E. P. Dutton published *High, Wide*

And Handsome under the pseudonym Curt Brandon. The pseudonym was necessary because Macmillan claimed it owned all rights to the Curtis Bishop name for book publication. *Bugles Wake* by Curt Brandon followed, published by E. P. Dutton in 1952. *Rio Grande* under the byline Curtis Bishop was published in 1961 by Avalon Books, the last of his Western novels. Living in Austin, Texas, for much of his life, where he was able to study many of the documents of early Texas on deposit at the University of Texas' Special Collections, Bishop's Western fiction is informed by a faithfulness to factual history and authentic backgrounds for his characters, while he also was able to invest his stories with action and a good deal of dramatic excitement.

Center Point Publishing
600 Brooks Road • PO Box 1
Thorndike ME 04986-0001 USA

(207) 568-3717

US & Canada:
1 800 929-9108
www.centerpointlargeprint.com